Old Tim's Estate

The Eddie Devlin Compendium

Old Tim's Estate

DISCARDED

T. R. St. George

NORMANDALE COMMUNITY COLLEGE
LIBRARY
9700 FRANCE AVENUE SOUTH
BLOOMINGTON, MN 55431-4399

Copyright © 2000 by T.R. St. George.

Library of Congress Number: 00-192109
ISBN #: Softcover 0-7388-3716-4

All rights reserved. No part of this book may be reproduced or transmitted in any form or by any means, electronic or mechanical, including photocopying, recording, or by any information storage and retrieval system, without permission in writing from the copyright owner.

Cover, from left, Eddie Devlin, Buddy Douglas and Margie Bremer

This is a work of fiction. Names, characters, places and incidents either are the product of the author's imagination or are used fictitiously, and any resemblance to any actual persons, living or dead, events, or locales is entirely coincidental.

This book was printed in the United States of America.

To order additional copies of this book, contact:
Xlibris Corporation
1-888-7-XLIBRIS
www.Xlibris.com
Orders@Xlibris.com

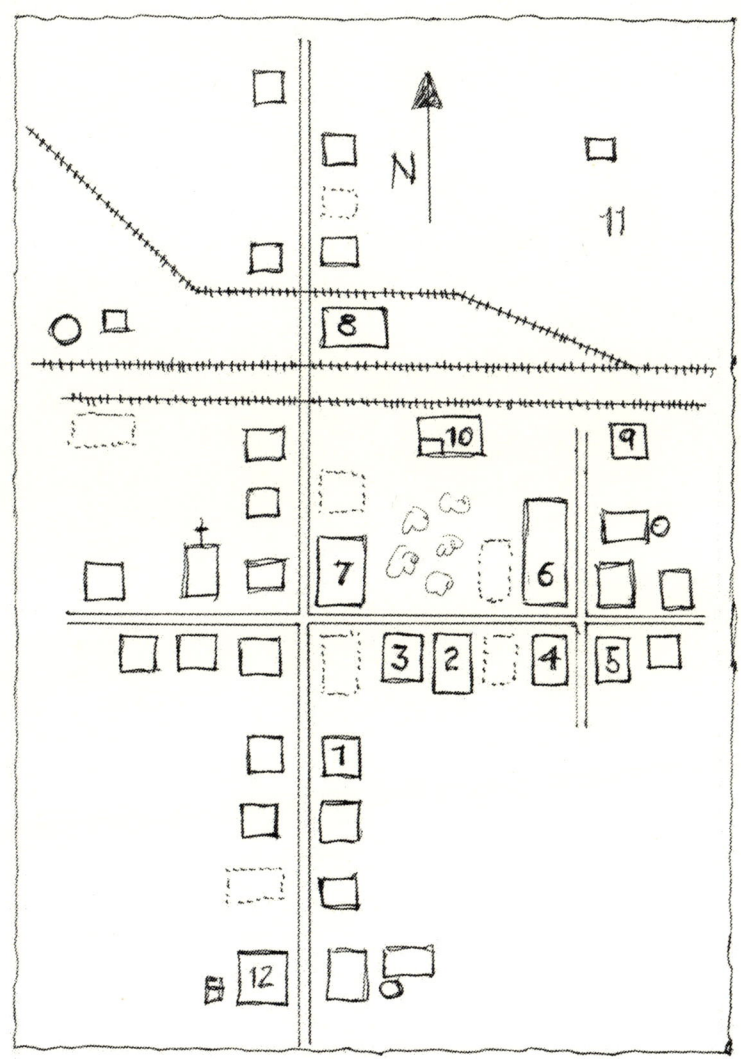

Old Tim's Estate (1929-35)

Stiles, 1929. (1) Devlins' house (2) Hack's garage (3) Poolhall (4) Al's Repair Shop (5) Claude Clarke's store (6) Lumberyard (7) Stiles Hotel (8) MSP&P Depot (9) Section Gang shack (10) Elevator (11) Lenny Gibbons' pasture (12) School. Dotted lines locate terminal fires.

For Silvana and Poppy

"I GUESS YOU DON'T HAVE TO LIVE IN A BIG CITY, YOU WANT TO ENCOUNTER SIN AND SOME LIFE'S TRAGEDIES. WE GOT PLENTY RIGHT HERE IN LITTLE OLD STILES."
—FRANK PRATT, SPEAKING FROM EXPERIENCE:
35 YEARS IN THE POOLHALL BUSINESS.

1.

On Friday, November 8, 1929, around five o'clock in the afternoon, Estelle Heaney—Timothy J. Heaney's oldest daughter, then twenty-six, single, still living at home, pretty much the custom until she's married if ever she is, presumed to be a virgin, the bookkeeper at S. Dolan & Sons Wholesale Groceries in Winatchee Falls—phones her Aunt Ceil Devlin nee Heaney in Stiles. Winatchee Falls is a small southern Minnesota city on both banks of the meandering Winatchee River, est. pop. 22,000-plus but that's a Chamber of Commerce est. Stiles is an unincorporated dot on the prairie ten miles to the southeast. So this is a long-distance call the Operator at the telephone company puts through. It costs thirty cents, which Estelle charges to S. Dolan & Sons. Old Sam Dolan, though Estelle sometimes phones Claude Clarke's General Store in Stiles on legitimate grocery business, might catch this minor misfeasance and raise hell. But old Sam's not around much any more since felled by a stroke during the August heat wave and when he is, all bundled up in his wheelchair, no longer knows who Estelle is. Neither Son, Woodrow or Wilson, is smart enough to catch it. They leave the bookkeeping and the long-distance charges to Estelle.

The Operator puts the call through. The phone rings, a long ring and three short rings, at the Devlins' modest home in Stiles and Ceil Devlin gets up from her afternoon rest on the couch in the living room, also the dining room—Ceil's said to be "high strung" and thought to be "not well"—and goes to the phone on the wall beside the bay window. This phone is an oak box somewhat larger than a shoebox with a black protruding mouthpiece and a receiver on a hook on its side. Ceil lifts the receiver from its hook and shouts (she and many others believe shouting improves the telephone service) into the mouthpiece, "Hello."

Ceil's only child, Edward (Eddie) Temperance Devlin, nine going on ten, Ceil's forty-six, arrives home at this instant, banging through the backdoor into the kitchen, where his Aunt Bee (Ceil's sister, two years older than Ceil, never married, she lives with the Devlins, does the cooking and pretty much runs the house) is baking bread in the cast iron stove at which she spends half her waking life. Eddie heads for the kitchen sink. There's a small pump with a curved iron handle beside this sink that lifts water from a cistern in the cellar. This is "washing water." It's not potable: worms and things live in the cistern. Everybody bathes in it though after Bee heats a pailful to near boiling on the cast iron stove, a once-a- week Saturday night bath in a washtub in the little room off the kitchen in which Bee does the laundry. Drinking water, called "well water," comes out of a similar but larger pump on a concrete slab in the backyard beside Bee's big vegetable garden, which, that pump, sometimes freezes solid in the winter, in which case Bee has to prime it with boiling water.

Eddie pumps an inch of washing water into the kitchen sink, scrubs his hands though not much and splashes water on his hair, face, denim shirt and bib overalls.

"You're washing!" Bee, evincing surprise, says.

"Got my hands dirty," Eddie says. He spent the afternoon after school let out at three-thirty and he changed his clothes with his best friend, Robert (Buddy) Douglas, likewise nine, climbing on the boxcars, gondolas and flat cars the Milwaukee St. Paul & Pacific Railroad parks on its long spur track in Stiles, running on top of the boxcars, fearlessly leaping from one to another. This is forbidden by Ceil, she's afraid Eddie will fall and get killed, but Eddie does it anyway. All the nine-year-old boys in Stiles and some younger and Margie Bremer,

Old Tim's Estate

a girl not quite nine, do it. Eddie spent the rest of the afternoon, this also forbidden by Ceil, smoking roll-your-owns with Buddy in an empty open boxcar. Buddy'd filched cigarette papers and a sack of Bull Durham from his big brother Ronnie's pants and first tried to sell Eddie the smokes he rolled, Eddie's not learned that manly art, but finally agreed to share them when it turned out he had no matches and Eddie had no money but had matches, a dozen Diamond matches filched from Bee's kitchen. Eddie sometimes likes to set fires.

But it's water Eddie needs now, not fire, and he splashes more washing water on his hair, shirt and bib overalls in an effort to kill the smell of cigarettes and smoke, which Ceil, she's got a nose like a bloodhound, can detect at fifty paces. Between splashes, though not much interested, he listens to Ceil's end of the conversation on the phone. It's somewhat cryptic, often the case. The Devlins and everybody else with a phone in Stiles (population 102 counting Miss Mott, the teacher who stays with the Boettchers) are on a party-line, thirteen parties, and rubbernecking, listening to other party's phone conversations, is a popular indoor sport.

"No," Ceil says, "Why? What? Well, I suppose. Maybe. But I think Henry's picked all the corn. What? I can't hear you, Estelle. I think somebody's on the line." This veiled accusation won't discourage any rubberneckers. "What? Tonight? Well, I suppose so. Probably. I'll have to ask Hack." Hack Devlin, her husband, Eddie's father. "Yes, about eight, I suppose. We still have Frank and Ernie, you know. Yes, it will be nice to see you."

Eddie lets the water out of the sink, it drains into the ground under the cellar, and hopes for the best, smellwise. Ceil comes into the kitchen, where Bee's taking four loaves of fresh-baked bread out of the cast iron stove. Ceil's tall and thin like her late father, Old Tim Heaney. Bee's short and round-shouldered like her late mother, the former Mary Clark. Ceil, before she married Hack Devlin and they settled in Stiles, was a teacher in one-room country schools for ten years, teaching everything from the ABCs to square roots, and frequently facing down large mutinous farm boys half again her size.

T.R. St. George

Then for two years she taught the Eighth Grade at Holy Redeemer Elementary in Winatchee Falls. She wasn't a nun like the other Holy Redeemer teachers ("Next damn thing to one though," Hack's brother Dick, the best man at their wedding, is said to have said at the wedding reception) but no nun wanted the Eighth Grade, full of adolescents beset by puberty. Ceil still acts like a teacher sometimes and sometimes seems to wish she still was one.

"That was Estelle on the phone," Ceil says, "She wondered if we'd seen Tim. Wondered did he stop by. She thinks he might gone out to the farm to see Henry and look at the corn. Why would he do that? Corn's all picked anyway, isn't it? And she wants us to come in and have cake and coffee with them tonight. We'll have to eat early if we do. Or leave something for Frank and Ernie. Hack'll have to shave. What do you think? Should we? We don't get a whole lot of invitations there."

"Be nice to see the girls," Bee says, meaning Estelle and her little sister Edith. Timothy J. Heaney's other daughters, Edna and Edwina, are married and long gone. Henry's another Heaney sibling, the farming Heaney.

"I'd like to," Eddie, casting another ballot, says. His Uncle Tim Heaney owns an insurance agency and, enormously rich by Eddie's standards, practically a millionaire, sometimes slips Eddie a quarter when their paths cross.

"Maybe we should," Ceil says, "Estelle sounded sort of, well, funny. Peculiar. I think she has something on her mind. I can't imagine what. But she called long-distance."

"Dolans will pay for that," Bee says, "You know Estelle." Nevertheless, that's something to think about. Long-distance calls in Stiles (and in Winatchee Falls, just about everywhere in the Devlins' and Bee's experience) are reserved for major disasters. Deaths, usually.

"I think we should," Ceil, making a command decision, says. "I smell cigarettes! Edward! Were you smoking!"

"No, no!" Eddie, a practiced liar, halfway out the kitchen door, says. "It's just Buddy was and he prolly blew smoke on me. I got to fix my bike, the chain—"

Old Tim's Estate

"Never mind your bike," Ceil says, "Go tell your dad to close up early and come home. He'll have to shave if we're going to the Heaneys. And tell Frank and Ernie we'll be eating early, quarter to six."

Eddie departs, grabs his bike from beside the backdoor, there's nothing wrong with the chain, another lie, and heads for Stiles' main street on the dirt path, there's been no snow yet, that crosses the vacant lot beside the Devlins' house.

Frank and Ernie. Frank Pratt owns and runs Stiles' one-table poolhall next-door to Hack Devlin's garage and two-pump gas station on main street. Ernie Hoff's the manager at the Frohoeft Lumber Co. lumberyard, also on main street. Frank boards at the Devlins, eats dinner at noon and supper at six o'clock except supper Sundays, charged $6 a week because he's a big eater. (Lunch in Stiles is a sandwich, some fruit and a piece of cake or something in a paper sack or a lunch bucket people take to work or school.) Ernie rooms-and-boards at the Devlins, three meals a day, he has the big bedroom, charged $12 a week.

Ceil Devlin doesn't much like these arrangements, launched four years ago when Ernie came to town and needed a place to live and Mrs. Boettcher was sick for awhile and couldn't board Frank any more. Ernie bores Ceil and Frank frequently "irritates" her. But the Devlins need the money and Bee doesn't mind the extra work. Bee likes to cook and feed people and thinks Frank "good company." He's always full of news, rumors, information and misinformation he gleans from customers at his poolhall and likes to share this news.

Frank's a big man in his fifties (6-2, 250 pounds) with a big hard belly Bee calls his "corporation," never married, with an Old Glory tattooed on his left forearm, his contribution to the Allied Cause during The Big War. This flag sort of waves when he makes a fist and his arm muscles bulge. Frank's prone to make every now and then, these irritating Ceil, major philosophical pronouncements based on his thirty-five years in the poolhall business. He was the day manager at Black's Billiards in Winatchee Falls before, he wanted a place of his

T.R. St. George

own, he bought the poolhall in Stiles in 1923, though it wasn't a poolhall then. It was Butch Ringey's failed feed store, a good-sized stucco building with one big window overlooking main street. Frank sold the feed Butch left in it cheap. He had a sign made, Frank's Billiards & Refreshments, it hangs over the door, and hung a curtain, it's pretty dirty now, in the big window, so people passing by can't look in and see who's in the poolhall. He put shelves and a counter and a big metal cooler that holds ice in big chunks the Tastee Bread truck delivers and two used restaurant tables and some beat-up chairs and a pot-bellied stove in the front part and a used pool table he bought from Black's at a good price in back. The Refreshments are ice cream, pop, Prohibition near beer, candy bars, licorice sticks, red or black, and tobacco products: cigarettes, cigars and chewing tobacco, Skoal and Red Dog, in plugs and little cans. Frank's also thought to do a little bootlegging on the side. That's illegal but practically a cottage industry ten years into Prohibition and only the Drys (Ceil's one of those) think it's really a crime. Mainly, though, the poolhall is Stiles' community center, Men Only, a free-for-all forum for a wide assortment of wide-ranging views on numerous subjects the ancient Greeks, Socrates and his pupils, might envy. Or might not. Frank's not mean to kids but he doesn't like them hanging around either if they're not buying anything. He sometimes lets Eddie though.

 Frank sleeps in a little room partitioned off behind the pool table, close to his back door and the path through the weeds to the outdoor privy he shares with Hack Devlin's garage. He makes his own breakfast, coffee he boils on the pot-bellied stove, and afterwards, usually, shoots a few racks, just to keep his hand in. Frank doesn't actually play much pool. He's a pool shark, will only play for money, as much as two-bits a game, and nobody in or near Stiles will play him any more because, though he spots them four or five balls, he always wins. He sometimes takes fifty cents off a stranger passing through. On Sunday nights, unless there's a blizzard or something, he turns the poolhall over to Banty Shanahan, his best customer, drives to Winatchee Falls

Old Tim's Estate

in his '24 Studebaker and dines with a mysterious lady friend thought to be a rich widow. He's usually sort of tired and mopy Mondays.

Ernie Hoff, likewise single, is a humorless German in his mid-thirties, built low to the ground, thought to be "thick," meaning not very bright, and "tight" with his money. He's often the butt of jokes at the poolhall. When on rare occasions he opens his wallet, attached to his belt with a chain, to buy a bottle of pop or near beer, Banty Shanahan if present and Banty usually is always hoots, "Hey! A maut juss flew out that!"

"Hey, a maut just flew out that!"

This Irish wit goes right over Ernie's humorless German head. Nevertheless, Ernie fancies himself an aeronautical engineer and is building an airplane, has been since late June—he saw the blueprints advertised for $12.95 in Air Aces Magazine and sent away for them—in Al Morris' Repair Shop, though Al and Hack Devlin are doing most of the actual work. Hack, a first-class auto mechanic, is "hotting up" in his garage the used Model T Ford engine that will power the airplane. Al's a skinny young fellow in his mid-twenties who likes to tinker with things. Skilled as a brain surgeon with his welding torch, he repairs farm machinery and just about anything else that's broken except automobiles: he leaves those to Hack. Ceil Devlin frequently says Hack and Al are "wasting valuable time fooling around with Ernie's silly airplane." But the airplane's first flight in the probable near future with Ernie at the controls has all Stiles waiting, the betting at the poolhall around six-to-five the airplane won't get off the ground.

Eddie delivers his messages. Hack Devlin (a second surviving son baptized Hackney Edward, Edward because he had to have a saint's name, Hackney a name selected nobody knows why by Granny Devlin, the only human being who ever calls him that) says, All right, he'll close up early, he's still waiting on a part for the confounded Hupmobile he's overhauling anyway. Frank and Ernie also say sure, eating early is fine with them and, his errands run, Eddie rides home on his bike, planning ways to spend the quarter his Uncle Tim Heaney may slip him.

The early supper is salmon patties, boiled potatoes, some green beans Bee canned and a lemon pie she baked. Catholics who hope to see Heaven have to eat fish on Fridays and Frank and Ernie, boarding with Catholics though they're both some kind of non-practicing Protestants, likewise eat fish on Fridays. Eddie sometimes wonders: will eating fish on Fridays give Frank and Ernie a slim shot at Heaven? Probably not. They're Protestants, already forever dammed. He has that on good authority, the word of the True Church.

Then it's time he prepares for the visit with the Timothy J. Heaneys, washes ("Wash good!" Ceil tells him) and gets all dressed up. All dressed up—that's the way they say it in the Middle West, where people with no clothes on are said to be "bare naked" and things that are new are "brand new."

Old Tim's Estate

For nearly fifty years, Timothy J. Heaney, the J for Jeremiah, the first surviving son born to Old Tim Heaney and the former Mary Clarke in 1875, was Young Tim Heaney. Then, when Old Tim died at eighty, he became plain Tim, though preferring Timothy. Old Tim Heaney when Young Tim was the first surviving son of a rawboned hard-drinking Pittsburgh trolley-car conductor born in County Cork then known as Old Tim, both their given names as was the Irish custom that of their paternal grandfathers. Old Tim the trolley-car conductor was a drinker and when drinking liked to beat his wife and eight offspring. In the summer 1862 then Young Tim, just turned eighteen, fed up with beatings and life in Pittsburgh and the Civil War underway, quit his job at the coal company and enlisted for nine months in the 21st Pennsylvania Infantry, raised hastily to confront General Robert E. Lee and the Confederates then ranging north into Maryland. Young Tim did his nine months, drilling a lot and pulling many details, saw brief action in a skirmish with some Confederate cavalry and was mustered out in the spring of '63. Back in Pittsburgh, he had a bare-knuckle fight with Old Tim that went fourteen rounds to a draw, then left home again, permanently, heading for what then was considered The West with his Enlistment Bonus: the right to homestead eighty acres just about anywhere west of the Mississippi River.

Young Tim took passage on a keelboat down the Ohio to Cincinnati, walked across the rest of Ohio, Indiana and Illinois with some Swedes bound for Iowa in two Conestoga wagons, learning to help with the horses, replaced a drunken deck hand on a steamboat bound upriver in Galena, Illinois, jumped ship in Winona, Minnesota, walked some more and eventually selected eighty acres in Winatchee County, where many say the Great Prairie begins. He filed his homestead in Winatchee Falls, the county seat platted by a visionary Yankee in 1854 beside a three-foot drop (the falls) in the Winatchee River, "Winatchee" an Indian word meaning, it's thought, either "slow water" or "wild gooseberries."

Young Tim bought a secondhand horse and harness for $8 from

an earlier homesteader named Schermerhorn and a tent and an ax and provender in Winatchee Falls, pitched his tent and spent the summer clearing his eighty of scattered trees, mostly oak and red maple, and the hard round stones called niggerheads left by the last Great Glacier, piling the stones in a gully—back-breaking work but Young Tim was rawboned like Old Tim the trolley-car conductor, chock full of pioneer spirit and blessed with lots of stamina. He'd learned to swing an ax building breastworks and to brew coffee and cook salt pork and beans in a frying pan over an open fire while a private in the 21st Pennsylvania.

Summer over, Young Tim built a small log cabin with a niggerhead fireplace, Schermerhorn and other neighbors helping him as was the custom, then, his cash exhausted, hired out to other homesteaders, mainly Irish who'd escaped the potato famine and Germans dodging service in the Kaiser's army, within easy riding distance on his secondhand horse. He soon was known as a "good worker" though a teetotaler, a failing viewed with suspicion by many Irish, but he'd seen enough of drink and drunkenness and the evils associated therewith in Pittsburgh and the 21st Pennsylvania. He saved most of his earnings, bought a plow and a scythe in the spring, raised and sold in '64 at good wartime prices a good crop, wheat and oats, came to the conclusion he could work more land and enlisted again, becoming a replacement in the Second Minnesota Infantry and presently, in view of his previous service, a corporal. He saw no action, however, before General Robert E. Lee surrendered at Appomattox, his only war stories that brief skirmish with Rebel cavalry and the sad bitter day the Second Minnesota stood with the massed Honor Guard at Abraham Lincoln's funeral in the nation's capital. Mustered out again shortly thereafter, he soon was back in Winatchee County with his Enlistment Bonus.

Land at the edge of the Great Prairie still was as endless and almost as empty as the sea. Young Tim homesteaded another eighty acres adjoining his first eighty, thus becoming a major agriculturist, cleared that eighty of trees and niggerheads and hired out through

Old Tim's Estate

two more winters. In the autumn of '68, by which time he owned a team and wagon and had harvested and sold three more crops, he and his neighbors raised near the log cabin a barn built with sawed lumber and he bought six Holstein heifers and married Mary Clark, seventeen: her father Jeremiah's eighty acres adjoined his first eighty. In 1874 Young Tim and Mary abandoned the log cabin, turning it into a shed, and had built for $600 in cash a good-sized frame house, white with green trim, with a "storm cellar" under it, case a cyclone came through, and a big yard overlooking the new road the county was putting through between their eighties.

Throughout these years and all their subsequent years Young Tim and the former Mary Clark were staunch members of the Precious Blood Parish established in 1855, the name a compromise imposed by the diocesan bishop after sundry Irish lobbying for St. Bridget's and sundry Germans touting St. Karl's came to blows at a parish meeting. The first church was a log structure on a low hill a mile from the Heaney farm on the track the new county road followed. When a permanent stone church with a bell tower and high arched windows was built on the same site in 1875, Young Tim Heaney was selected to make the six-day round-trip to Winona with a team-and-wagon to pick up the stained glass windows, he being one of perhaps three parishioners thought likely to make that trip and return sober with the windows unbroken. A year later Young Tim became plain Tim following Old Tim the trolley-car conductor's death during a bout with the DTs, this information arriving by post a month after the event.

Throughout these years and more, Tim and Mary, as a later Pope frequently would exhort all good Catholics to do, procreated with evident vigor, adding several souls to the Precious Blood parish roles and Cemetery: Nell and Gert (born in the log cabin and proud of that in later years), a Young Tim who died at birth, the Young Tim who survived, plain Tim then becoming Old Tim, two girls who died in infancy, Beatrice (Bee from birth), Ceil, another boy dead at three with the whooping cough, and Henry, a late-comer in 1893.

T.R. St. George

The surviving Young Tim, though the hundred-and-sixty acres would have been his since he was the oldest son, evinced no interest in agriculture as a boy or youth. He wished instead to go to high school in Winatchee Falls, by then a metropolis with close to 9,000 inhabitants, and Old Tim, following some soul-searching, let him, paying for his room-and-board, $6 a week in a respectable boarding house, though making him help with the farm work summers, which Young Tim detested. Young Tim was tall for the times like Old Tim, five-ten, but smaller boned, and his hands never grew calloused, only blistered. He didn't tan either, just turned pink when out in the sun. Three summers of that were enough for Young Tim. He got a job selling shoes at Knowlton's Department Store in Winatchee Falls, dropped out of high school and, his remittance promptly terminated, began to pay his own room-and-board. He subsequently sold men's clothing at Madden's Menswear in Winatchee Falls (becoming a very sharp dresser himself who always wore spats, stiff white detachable collars and a fake pearl tie-pin), took night classes, got his high school diploma and discovered his true calling, which was selling insurance, Life Fire & Casualty, for the Adolph Mensch Insurance Agency.

In 1902 at age twenty-seven, following a difference of opinion regarding commissions with old Adolph Mensch, Young Tim launched his own agency, Heaney Life Fire & Casualty, in Winatchee Falls, and was deemed a true success by all who knew him, including Old Tim, though some of the shine and glitter came off that a month later when Young Tim married one Bergda Sorensen, a Norwegian woman he met at an insurers' convention in Des Moines, Iowa, whose father also was in the insurance business. Bergda was a Protestant! A Lutheran or something. They were married by a priest, Father O'Herlihy at Holy Redeemer, but not in the church, in the sacristy. It took the rest of the Heaneys a long time to get over that. Mary Heaney never did get over it altogether and said a Rosary every day for the rest of her life for the eventual repose of Young Tim's immortal soul. But Bergda, though declining to convert, she wasn't much of a church-goer herself, agreed pre-nuptially to raise the kids Catholic if there

Old Tim's Estate

were any (there soon were the four girls) and in time the Heaneys accepted her. More or less. Young Tim meanwhile put the shine back on his reputation. He sold Dr. Wayne Pretzell—a visionary chiropractor out from Philadelphia who (joined later by his chiropractor brothers, Ward and Waverly) founded the soon somewhat famous Pretzell Chiropractic Clinic in Winatchee Falls in 1900—the first automobile policy issued in Winatchee County, collision and liability on a Stanley Steamer Hawk. At which point Heaney Life Fire & Casualty became Heaney Life Fire Casualty & Auto and hired its first salesman, Young Matt Malloy, paying Matt commissions against a $10-a-week draw.

And the years rolled by. Old Tim and Henry the late-comer, who always liked farming and thus escaped the World War I draft, farmers considered essential, worked the hundred-and-sixty until 1920, when Walter married Emma Schloss and Old Tim retired at seventy-six, though still helping with the harvest and the corn-picking, and moved with Mary into a tiny frame house, two stories, two bedrooms and a storage space upstairs, they had built, paid for in cash, in Stiles, a village platted in 1888 a mile east of the Precious Blood church. Old Tim by then owned a set of the Encyclopedia Britannica (purchased in part because he felt he lacked education, in part to help Mary's worthless brother Emmett, who was trying with faint success to sell Britannicas door-to-door) and had read the whole set, cover-to- cover, it took him fourteen years, though admittedly skimming some subjects. He also was a founding member and twice past-president of the Winatchee County Temperance Union, a former two-term State Representative (elected by the Drys in 1918 but defeated by a Wet in '22, Prohibition already proving a disaster), a former commander of the Winatchee County Veterans of the Grand Army of the Republic (of whom thirty or so, Old Tim among them, some a bit shaky, still marched in the Memorial Day, Fourth of July and Armistice Day parades in Winatchee Falls) and a partner with Claude Clarke in a cheese factory on Stile's main street, though his wife Mary didn't think much of that endeavor.

T.R. St. George

The Clarkes with an "e" (Mary Heaney nee Clark when alive and other Clarks without an "e" frequently noted) were a thin branch of the Clarks without an "e" in County Kilkenny, second cousins once removed or something. The Clarkes' first immigrant ancestor, however, Old John Clark, so the story goes, added the "e" when queried by the Immigration at Ellis Island, a sneaky move many Clarks without an "e" three generations later still consider a vain attempt to achieve sudden upward mobility, the Immigration and others in America then thinking Clarkes with an "e" Lace Curtain Irish and Clarks without an "e" Shanty Irish. Clarkes with an "e" also are adverse to "hard work," or so Eddie truly believes, numerous Clarks without an "e" having told him that. Few Clarkes with an "e" are farmers at any rate and those who are generally are thought to be and seem to be failures at farming. Clarkes with an "e," of whom there are by now a considerable number in Winatchee County, prefer "soft jobs" or business ventures and seem to do better at those. Claude Clarke, Old Tim's partner in the cheese factory, is one shining example. Just what the simple sneaky addition of a single vowel has to do with all this is a mystery, at least to Eddie: nevertheless, he considers it a true fact.

Mary Heaney was carried off by a massive stroke in the Winter of '22, age seventy-one. Eddie but dimly remembers her. The cheese factory, often the case with fledgling business ventures in Stiles, burned to the ground a year later, nothing left of it now but a hole full of rusty tanks and ancient ashes sprouting weeds, mainly burdocks, between Hack Devlin's garage and Al's Repair Shop. Eddie remembers that fire or thinks he does, flames leaping high in the night, all the able-bodied men in Stiles heaving useless buckets of water, Ceil crying because Old Tim's business was going up in smoke and she was afraid Hack's garage would go too and it wasn't insured, Hack having spent his life savings and $300 Old Tim loaned him to buy the garage for $500. But the garage was a brick building and the bucket brigade, giving up on the cheese factory, drenched its tarpaper roof and saved it. The Devlins were living then in two second-floor rooms with cooking privileges in Lee J. Lilly's Stiles Hotel across main street

Old Tim's Estate

and Eddie watched the fire and the inept fire-fighters from a window, or thinks he did. It's one of his earliest memories if in fact he remembers it, but he may be confused. Another blaze some months earlier destroyed Dan Bailey's Livery Stable on main street, Al's Repair Shop is there now, and there have been other fires since: Peterson's Grocery Store, Young Billy McBride's house, one of the Midwest Milling Co. grain elevators, the other one still stands. Fires in Stiles, there's no real way to fight them, usually burn to the ground whatever it is they're burning.

The Baileys, the Petersons and the McBrides, Young Billy was the elevator manager, moved from Stiles following their fires. Old Tim Heaney did not, though pretty much fully retired after the cheese factory burned, and neither did Claude Clarke. The cheese factory was insured: Young Tim Heaney wrote the policy. Claude Clarke (a second son like Hack Devlin, neither Old nor Young) opened his grocery store with his share of the insurance money and attained a local monopoly when Peterson's Store burned. A sturdy local joke is Claude set that fire. Claude also got the new Post Office then, the old one at Peterson's gone up in smoke, and became Stiles' Postmaster, space in his store equipped by the Government, and soon launched a cream route as well. His son Fred (Poop) Clarke, nineteen, handles the cream route, out every morning at five a.m. in his new 1926 Ford truck to pick up milk and cream at twenty-odd farms and deliver same to the Winatchee Falls Co-op Dairy. Poop's also a second son. His big brother, one of several John Clarkes in Winatchee County, sells roofing at the Frohoeft Lumber Co. lumberyard in Winatchee Falls. Claude Clarke is Stiles' leading entrepreneur.

Pneumonia contracted while helping Henry pick corn took Old Tim off in the fall of 1924. The wake, it lasted three days, was held at his house in Stiles, "wake" a funny word for it Eddie thought then and thinks still since half the people present said Old Tim looked "just like he's sleeping, Danny Malone did a good job on him." Many stories extolling Old Tim's virtues and insignificant vices were told during the three days. Eddie listened to some of them and ate a lot of chocolate cake and other stuff provided by relatives and neighbors and (though Ceil and Bee and his Aunt Nell and Aunt Gert cried a lot) had a pretty good time, all things considered, playing hide-and-seek etc. with his numerous cousins, mostly Devlins, and the other kids present. He wore his new suit, his first suit, "handed down" from his cousin Mickey Devlin, to Old Tim's funeral at the Precious Blood church. Which he mainly remembers because Mame McCready—a good-looking woman in her mid-twenties already launched on a vocal career, singing weekends with a band based in Winatchee Falls, her virtue consequently suspect—sang at it, pumping the old organ up in the choir loft and screeching "Nearer My God to Thee." Her dad, old Mac McCready, a squat old man with bristly eyebrows whose two-hundred acres said to be heavily mortgaged adjoined the Heaney farm, volunteered Mame's talent and, while Mame pumped and screeched, glared at those present who did not appear moved by her performance or looked doubtful of her virtue.

Old Tim Heaney was buried beside Mary and their several dead offspring in the Precious Blood Cemetery in front of a big red granite tombstone with Heaney and their names and life spans except Old Tim's, that still to come, on it. Aunt Gert, often thought to be a little flaky, thought they should bury with Old Tim his favorite Britannica volume, I to Izaat, the one with the History of Ireland, but Ceil Devlin said that would spoil the set and the idea was abandoned. Everybody stood to windward of the grave, hunched up, their backs to a cold November wind sweeping across the bare brown fields, while Father Callahan mumbled prayers in Latin and splashed holy water on Old Tim's casket and a few mourners. Eddie watched the actual burial wide-eyed, Old Tim's casket sinking slowly and with great finality on straps manipulated by Danny Malone the undertaker and his brother Sean into the grave Banty Shanahan dug. It's the first funeral and burial Eddie really remembers. His other grandfather, Old Ed Devlin, died before he was born: Young Ed got the farm. Granny Devlin's eighty-something but still going strong. She lives with her daughter Kate and Kate's husband, Loren Erdman, he

Old Tim's Estate

works for the city, in Winatchee Falls. Eddie also cried a little, Ceil and all his aunts were and his Uncle Tim and Uncle Henry were sort of wiping their eyes, and was truly sorry for a time that his grandfather Old Tim Heaney was dead and on his way to Heaven, that the assumption anyway. Old Tim, though a stern disciplinarian with all his descendants, sometimes dispensed nickels with the understanding the descendants so rewarded would grow up to be teetotalers.

It was Banty Shanahan, irrepressible even at graveside, used to graves from digging them and waiting to shovel dirt into this one, who noted the passing of another generation. "Well, Young Tim Heaney," Banty said, "I guess yer juss plain Tim now." And so it was and is, though surviving members of Old Tim's generation still call and will always call Timothy J. Heaney "Young Tim."

Old Tim's estate, considering he'd set aside $300 for his funeral expenses and started with two Enlistment Bonuses, $40 saved while in the 21st Pennsylvania and Second Minnesota and $50 in mustering-out pay, was not inconsiderable: the one-hundred-sixty acres, free and clear, no mortgage, with good buildings and pretty good machinery, $15,200 including the cheese factory insurance in a savings account in the First National Bank of Winatchee Falls and the house in Stiles, likewise free and clear, no mortgage, in which he and Mary spent their last days, cared for by Bee, and a complete set of the Encyclopedia Britannica, circa 1906. All of which Old Tim, having given these holdings considerable thought, bequeathed thus in his Last Will & Testament:

Henry Heaney got the hundred-and-sixty, title to same and all its chattels, though Bee so long as she is single "in view of her loving care" gets ten percent of the annual cash crop income if there is any. Ceil and Bee (Old Tim surmising that Hack Devlin, a first-class mechanic but a terrible businessman, everybody owes him, never would get enough money together to repay his $300 loan, let alone buy a house) got the house in Stiles in joint life tenancy or single tenancy should either die or move from it (the Devlins promptly moved into it), though title to the property remained with the estate. Old Tim, who hated bankers and mortgages and often while alive called bankers "dad-banged parasites," was afraid Hack if short of cash and Hack was always short of cash might talk Ceil and Bee into mortgaging the property. Hack's $300 loan was forgiven. Ceil also got the automobile, a 1922 Reo tourer Old Tim never really learned to drive, he left the driving to Ceil once she learned, but the Reo didn't amount to much. It rests with other abandoned early automotive experiments in the weeds behind Hack's garage, the engine blown, its canvas top in shreds, sparrows nesting in the spare tire. Hack often says he plans to overhaul it but he's not got around to that yet. The other daughters, Nell and Gert, got $2,500 each, Old Tim deeming their respective husbands, Wesley L. Kemp and Old Charlie Goggins, marginally competent providers: both were and still are employed by the B&P Meat Packing Co. in Fairbow, forty miles to the west across the prairie. Timothy J. Heaney got the Britannicas and "One Dollar ($1.00) in view of the fact that he is well able to provide for himself and his family." The balance in savings in the First National Bank, $10,199, Old Tim left "In trust to my children and their children should any require extensive medical treatment, the advanced schooling of the latter in the amount of $250 each provided they are of good character and remain teetotalers, or in the event of dire need."

Timothy J. Heaney, naturally, was named executor with authority to disburse such funds. None have been, however. No family member's required extensive medical treatment, no progeny to date has evinced any interest in advanced schooling (it's thought Old Tim meant high school or conceivably college) and everybody's got a roof over their heads and food on the table. Nobody's in dire need. And the $10,199, invested by Timothy J. Heaney in good sound railroad bonds at six percent per annum, amounts to more than $14,000 now. Timothy J. Heaney reports its growth annually at year-end.

Old Tim's Estate

All the Heaneys call this sum "The Estate" and it's like a lifeboat, watered and provisioned, unsinkable, always there should any family member ever need it. The Estate. Old Tim's legacy.

"Come in, come in! So nice you could come. My, Eddie, aren't you growing! You're quite the little man now!" Thus Estelle Heaney (skinny, flat-chested, her hair in a "permanent," Bee calls her a "nervous type," no beau in sight so far as anybody knows, getting on to be an old maid like Bee though Bee has a beau of sorts and vague prospects) greets the Devlins and Bee when they turn up at eight o'clock at Timothy J. Heaney's front door on West College Street in Winatchee Falls, a half-hour drive from Stiles on County Road O at a steady 25 mph in the Devlin's new car, an "enclosed" 1926 Model T Ford with windows that roll up and down Hack bought used a month ago for $135 at Cheesy Adams' Dodge-Plymouth dealership in Winatchee Falls, where his brother Dick Devlin is a salesman. The T needed new valves and a general overhaul but Hack got busy and fixed it and it purrs right along now.

Eddie Devlin, all the kids in Stiles, consider Winatchee Falls a true metropolis. Eddie knows, he's had geography, there are much bigger cities and he's been in one of them, St. Paul, once, for a day at the State Fair and a quick look at the State Capitol, just the outside: Ceil and Bee thought he should see the place in which his grandfather "helped make laws" while a member of State Legislature. But Winatchee Falls is metropolis enough. It has three movie theaters, two high schools (the Public and the Catholic), a whole bunch of restaurants, the Pretzell Chiropractic Clinic and its affiliated Chiropractic College, a big new fancy four-story hotel, The Dobermann, so named for its owner, old Hein (Dollar) Dobermann, Winatchee Falls leading entrepreneur, and there's a civic move afoot to sell bonds and build a Municipal Swimming Pool, match the grandeur of ancient Rome, because the Winatchee River is full of stuff dumped in it by the Co-op Dairy, posted No Swimming by the Health Department. The Pretzell Chiropractic Clinic, Eddie truly believes, is "world-famous" and "internationallly-known." That's what it says anyway, somewhat redundantly, in a brochure put out by the Winatchee Falls Chamber of Commerce, penned in part by the Clinic's founding brothers. No question though, year in and year out, The Chiro as it's locally known treats with varying degrees of success several thousand slipped discs, sagging sacroiliacs and other obscure medical problems. These patients come from all over the Corn Belt, the Dakotas and two Canadian provinces: that's where The Chiro's world-famous and internationally known. These transients are a big boost to Winatchee Falls' economy and many local residents gleefully fleece them for food, lodging and souvenirs during their sometimes lengthy stays.

The West Side is Winatchee Falls' classy side ("high-toned," Bee calls it) and West College Street is its premier residential street. The name, it first was West Center Street, dates to 1900 when for a time it was thought Winatchee Falls would get one of the State Teacher Colleges the Legislature was establishing, but Winatchee County's state representative proved an inept lobbyist and Winona got the Teachers College. The Pretzell Chiropractic Clinic and College, a complex of red-brick buildings, one like the Dobermann Hotel a towering four-stories, is on West College two blocks off Broadway: the Dobermann Hotel's across the street. Then West College over a distance of ten blocks climbs a low hill, the only hill in town, to Bluff Park, the top of the hill. All the houses on West College are massive by Eddie's standards: big frame houses, some three stories, in big yards full of trees. A few are brick houses and one at the top of the hill, Dr. Wayne Pretzell's house, is made of stone. Most of the yards are raked clean of leaves. People who live on West College, Eddie's heard but finds this hard to believe, pay people, men and half-grown boys, to rake their yards! A dozen chiropractors, other doctors who hate The Chiro and whine they're "real doctors," lawyers, a district judge, people who own stores or businesses or downtown buildings they rent, rich people, live in the big houses on West College, and the higher up they live the higher up they are in the scheme of things.

Timothy J. Heaney's house, a white frame two-story with a glassed-in

Old Tim's Estate

porch, another sign of wealth, is halfway up. Tim bought it two years ago, his insurance business booming, moving up from farther down when named a director at the First National Bank. This house has off-white wall-to-wall carpeting in the living room, which is furnished with a big soft couch and big stuffed chairs, a Silver Echo radio in a massive mahogany cabinet, two floor lamps, two table lamps bigger than milk cans on matching end-tables beside the big couch and a fancy breakfront with glass doors, its shelves jammed with crystal stuff. Tim's wife, Bergda the Lutheran, collects crystal: that's her hobby.

"Come in, come in," Estelle, she chatters like a squirrel, says. "Mother's upstairs. She'll be down in a just a minute. Edith's in the kitchen. She's making coffee. Oh, Eddie, be careful! There are leaves on your shoes!"

There were wet leaves on the sidewalk. Eddie picks the leaves off his new sneakers before setting foot on the wall-to-wall carpet as if entering a minefield. He's also wearing his second-best pants, bell-bottomed denims with a red elastic waistband called Whoopee pants, and a clean sportshirt and Bee after he washed himself scrubbed his ears and neck to a fare-the-well. He's under strict orders to "behave," he is behaving, but nervous Estelle makes him nervous. He picks his way across the living room minefield, through the dining room, where the Heaney's best china and more crystal nest behind glass, and into the kitchen. Edith, a plump blonde high school senior, placid like her mother Bergda, probably will give him a cookie or something. He rather likes Edith.

"Sit, sit," Estelle tells Ceil and Hack and Bee. "So good you all could come. Mother's upstairs. She'll be down in just a minute. Edith's making coffee."

"It was good of you to ask us," Ceil, settling on the big couch with Bee, says. "It's been awhile since we saw all of you."

In fact, it's been four months. These relatives last saw each other at the annual Fourth of July Picnic at Precious Blood, which the Timothy J. Heaneys always make a point of attending. So Tim can show off his new car, Ceil says, See his poor relations once a year then forget them. Tim buys his Buicks new, not used, another true measure of success.

"The weather's been good for this time of year," Hack Devlin, a master of small talk, says. He's a gaunt man in his late forties with a mechanic's battered knuckles and half a left little finger, the other half chopped off by a farm machine when he was fourteen, clean-shaven, with a nick on his chin, he shaves with a straight razor, shaved in a hurry, wearing worn brown oxfords and his only suit, a brown pinstripe shiny at the knees and elbows he bought On Sale at Montgomery Ward five years ago. He's sitting gingerly in one of the big stuffed chairs, pretending to be at ease, a poor relation by marriage who knows that. "Tim going pheasant hunting this year?"

"No, not this year," Estelle, plucking at her permanent, says. "You have to go all the way to South Dakota now to get any pheasants, he says, and that's too far. And he's breaking in a new agent. Training him. Old Matt Malloy's boy. Young Matt. I'll just run upstairs and tell mother you're here."

Estelle scoots up the stairs at the end of the living room and Ceil, Hack and Bee sit for a time in silence. Then Ceil points a finger at the big Silver Echo radio. "That's something new. I wonder how much it cost?"

"Hundred-sixty, seventy-five, my guess," Hack says, "Worth it though. Prolly gets stations all over the country."

The Devlins have a table-model Atwater-Kent radio Hack bought used at Rosen's Used Radios in Winatchee Falls, $2 down and $2 a week for twelve weeks, and hooked up to two six-volt car batteries since, practically speaking, there is no electricity in Stiles or anywhere out in the country, though the MSP&P depot, the Stiles Hotel, Frank Pratt's poolhall, Claude Clarke's store and Al's Repair Shop have gasoline generators and dim electric lights used sparingly. Most people have kerosene lamps. A few like the Devlins have gasoline lamps. Those cost more and their mantles, nine cents each, have to be replaced at intervals, but Ceil thinks kerosene lamps are "hard on the eyes, bad for reading." Ceil's a reader, she has a card at the

Old Tim's Estate

Winatchee Falls Public Library and gets books there, and hopes Eddie will be a reader too, some day. The Atwater-Kent mostly gets static but once late at night when Hack was fooling around with it he got—thinks he got anyway, heard the call letters—KDKA in Pittsburgh: a communications miracle.

Edith comes from the kitchen with Eddie, munching a cookie, in tow. Hack stands. "Hi," Edith says, "Aunt Ceil, Aunt Bee, Hack. It's nice to see you." She pecks Ceil and Bee on the cheek, shakes hands with Hack. "Coffee's perking. Just be a minute."

"Edward," Ceil says, "You're making crumbs. Eat that cookie in the kitchen." Eddie retreats to the kitchen as Bergda and Estelle come down the stairs. More greetings are exchanged, though Bergda, a big bosomy woman with blue eyes and a fat face, doesn't peck anybody's cheek. She's a cold-blooded Scandihoovian. Or maybe not, Hack Devlin thinks: she had three children in five years, Edith five years later. Hack sometimes wonders about other people's sex lives. His own scarcely exists: Ceil seldom "feels like it."

Conversation ensues. The current meteorological conditions are discussed. Likewise, the fact Henry Heaney had a good corn crop though corn unfortunately is fetching but 27 cents a bushel these days. Likewise, the fact that both the other Heaney girls, Edna and Edwina, are well and their husbands are doing well. Edna's, Warren Street, a veteran auto salesman fifteen years older than Edna, just bought the Nash dealership in Albuquerque, New Mexico, and Edwina's, Gil Foster, he works for the Federal Government in Boise, Idaho, something to do with Land Management, a good steady job, was recently promoted. Bee, queried, says Herb is fine. Herb is Herb Bender, Bee's beau. His farm, actually it's his mother's farm, adjoins the Precious Blood Cemetery. Herb and Bee have been "going together," they're sort of engaged, for ten years, waiting for old Mrs. Bender, who can't stand Bee and vice versa, to finally die and leave Herb the farm. Hack, also queried, says the airplane is "coming along pretty good." Word of Ernie Hoff's airplane-under-construction has spread far and wide but Hack would rather not discuss the airplane in Ceil's presence.

Edith, meanwhile, Eddie helping, sets the dining room table with the Heaneys' second-best china, a chocolate cake and coffee in an electric percolator. Edith seems sort of distracted but tells Eddie she plans to major in Home Ec when she goes to college, most likely St. Benedict's, then tells those in the living room, "Coffee's ready. Come try my cake."

All settle in the dining room. The coffee's poured, cream and sugar passed, the cake cut by Edith, served, tasted, praised.

"Edward, use your fork!" Ceil says, before Eddie starts eating his cake like a normal person, picking it up and stuffing it in his mouth. "Will Tim be joining us?"

"Uh, I don't think so," Estelle says, "He had to uh see a prospect."

"He had to uh go to a bank directors meeting," Bergda says. Then, suddenly, placid no longer, bursts into tears and chokes on her cake.

This unexpected development and the conflicting reports regarding Tim's whereabouts leave the Devlins and Bee confused and momentarily speechless while Estelle thumps Bergda's back. Bergda recovers, her big fat face bright pink. Big tears roll down her cheeks, cutting crooked channels through her powder.

"We don't know where Tim is!" Bergda blubbers, "He went to work this morning. Like he always does. Took his car. But he didn't go to his office. Peggy Connell, his office girl, called. She thought he might be sick or something and there was a man from The Prudential there, she said, wanted to see Tim. The District Manager. He had an appointment with Tim, he said. The District Manager said. Tim wasn't at the bank either. Or the Club. I called. Peggy said his car wasn't where he parks it. Behind the office. And he didn't come home for dinner! He's been gone all day and we don't know where he is! Tim's been under a lot of stress lately."

Bergda, she keeps Tim on a short leash, bursts into tears again, embarrassing everybody, and Estelle says, "Please, mother! Get hold of yourself!"

Old Tim's Estate

Dinner's the evening meal at the Heaneys and elsewhere on West College Street: it's supper as previously noted at the Devlins and elsewhere in Stiles and on farms. The Club is the Winatchee Falls Golf & Country Club. Tim doesn't golf, he'd turn pink in the sun, but he's a "social member" though not very sociable. Tim was a drinker for awhile in his early twenties when he was running around with Young Pat Madden and enjoying some normal rebellion, but Old Tim's temperance views were deep in his bones. All he drinks now is an occasional watery highball, but the Country Club social membership is good for his insurance business.

"Edward, go eat your cake in the kitchen," Ceil says, and Eddie takes his cake into the kitchen, where he stuffs it in his mouth while eavesdropping on the subsequent discussion in the dining room. Tim might had car trouble, Hack, who in a lifetime of driving used cars has had a lot of car trouble, says. But he'd phone if he did, Bergda says. Might be out in the country some place, Hack says, no phone handy. But he's been gone all day, Bergda blubbers, he might had an accident! We thought, Estelle says, he might gone out the farm, see Henry, look at the corn or something, but I called Henry, he wasn't there, corn's all picked anyway, Henry said. Well I wouldn't worry too much, Hack says, Tim's a growed man, he can take care of himself. But he's been under a lot of stress lately, Bergda blubbers, ever since the Stock Market—Was Tim, Ceil says, in the Stock Market? Well, yes, some, Estelle says, Bergda's still blubbering, he bought some stock, not very much, but you know Dad, he thinks he might lose a little money. How much, Ceil says, is not very much? Well we don't know exactly, Estelle says, two or three thousand dollars worth probably. Well that won't hurt Tim too much, Hack, a born optimist, says. But we think, Estelle says, he might been buying some stock on margin. I know, Bergda blubbers, Tim won't do anything foolish. But we don't know where he is! And he didn't come home for dinner! Did you, Ceil says, call Nell or Gert? No, not yet, Estelle says, but I don't think Dad'd go to Fairbow. Tim was going anywhere, Bergda blubbers, he'd tell me, he always does. Have some more cake everybody, Edith says, and there's plenty of coffee. Edith like Bee believes a full stomach solves most problems. Tell you what, Hack says, we'll drive slow our way home, take a look the ditches, just in case like you say Tim might went out the farm and had a little accident. We dint see anything our way in but we wasn't looking and anyway it was dark. Then I'll drive out the farm, take a look along the county road. Oh would you, Bergda blubbers, take the trouble, and phone us, call collect, I won't sleep a wink till you do! Sure thing, Hack says, no trouble uh tall. There there, Mother, Estelle says, she's blubbering some herself, don't worry, I'm sure Dad's all right, he'll turn up—Was Tim, Ceil says, doing pretty well in the Stock Market? Oh yes, very well, Estelle says, though I suppose The Crash.... more coffee, Hack? Just half a cup, Hack says, then maybe we better get going. Well why for heaven's sake, Estelle, Ceil says, didn't you tell me all this on the phone or tell us the minute we got here? Well I didn't want those dammed rubberneckers on your line knowing our business, Estelle says, and we thought Dad might come home or call so we'd just have some cake and coffee first.

The Full Stomach Theory at work. Also, the theory that these families, though not exactly close are nevertheless family, the logical support in times of crises.

Eddie, done with his cake, decides he'll ask, volunteer, to go along with his Dad and help look in the ditches along the county road for Uncle Tim's Buick. This strikes him as pretty exciting and, no school tomorrow, a good excuse to stay up past his usual bedtime, nine o'clock—if Ceil will let him.

The Stock Market CRASHED a week ago, made a big splash in the newspaper the Devlins get, the daily-except-Sunday Winatchee Falls Bugle Call, but had no more immediate impact on the Devlins or Bee or anybody else in Stiles than a distant earthquake in Afghanistan or somewhere, and it's still pretty much a mystery to Eddie. He first thought this CRASH meant the big building called The Stock Exchange there was a picture of in The Weekly Reader—in which, The Weekly Reader said, men in suits "made millions" buying and selling stock, whatever that is—had collapsed, killing or injuring many men

Old Tim's Estate

in suits, but now knows that was not the case. The Stock Exchange building still stands and the CRASH, whatever it was, seems to be blowing over. There have been other stories since in the Bugle Call anyway, Eddie sometimes skims the headlines on his way to the sports page, numerous big bankers pronouncing The Market, whatever that is, "fundamentally sound." The District 14 school get six primary Weekly Readers every week, which the kids share though some kids, fourth-graders even, Clyde Stoppel for one, really can't read them. Eddie can and does. The Weekly Reader, in fact, is pretty much his window on the world.

The only "stock" Eddie knows, however, is livestock: the pigs, cows and sheep Uncle Henry and other farmers drive in herds to and sometimes sell Saturdays at the Stiles Stockyard. Or sometimes they load this livestock into stinking trucks bound for the B&P Meat Packing Co. plant in Fairbow or stinking boxcars bound for the South St. Paul Stockyards. The Stiles Stockyard stinks too, pig poop's the worst, but Eddie and others Stiles kids often play there, nobody there usually except Saturdays. It's a good place to play, climb in and out of the pens, walk on the top rails if you're brave enough and have really good balance. Hinty Murphy, twelve, whose balance is phenomenal, can walk all the way around the Stockyard on the top rails, never falls off. Hinty can walk a rail on the MSP&P tracks, too, all the way through Stiles, never falls off.

"I simply don't understand it!" Ceil, for about the tenth time, says. "It's not like Tim. He always comes home for supper. Dinner, they call it. Or phones. Where could he possibly be? People don't just disappear! You don't suppose he was kidnapped? Somebody after his money?"

"Oh I doubt that," Hack says, "Tim's pretty well fixed, I guess. But kidnappers, they generally want like a million dollars ransom. Some figure like that. I doubt Tim's got that kind of money. My guess is he just went somewhere and had some car trouble. Or he might had a little accident. You see anything, Eddie?"

T.R. St. George

Eddie shakes his head. They're six miles out of Winatchee Falls on their way home in the Model T and Eddie's in the front seat with his head out the window, cranked down, scanning the ditch beside County Road O, just visible in the T's dim headlights. Hack's scanning the other ditch but they've seen no sign of any wrecked Buick.

"Roll your window up, Edward," Ceil says, "There's a draft back here. You can see through it." Eddie rolls the window up and presses his nose against the glass. "I had no idea Tim was fooling around in the Stock Market."

"Well, you know Tim," Bee says, "Johnny-on-the spot he thinks there's any money there. I don't know anything about the Stock Market."

"Buy cheap, sell dear," Hack, though he doesn't know much about the Stock Market either, says. All he knows is what he's heard, mostly uninformed and misinformed pronouncements at Frank Pratt's poolhall. "There's money to be made there all right. I expect Tim got his share."

So maybe, Eddie thinks, Uncle Tim was kidnapped. That's a pretty exciting idea. And right this very minute, Eddie's imagination slips into high gear, the kidnappers, four big ugly men with long criminal records, have Uncle Tim bound-and-gagged-tied-hand-and-foot somewhere while they write Aunt Bergda a Ransom Note. The somewhere probably is an old abandoned farmhouse. Like the old Forney place. Eddie's imagination goes into overdrive. He could sneak up on the kidnappers in the dark, he's reconnoitered the old Forney place with Buddy Douglas, dispatch one kidnapper with a blow to the throat with fingers extended, another with a kick in the groin though that location's a little hazy, the third with a hard chop on the back of his neck, the last one cringing then in fear of great bodily harm, and rescue Uncle Tim! Eddie's small for his age but wiry and he's studied the Judo book Ronnie Douglas saw advertised in Air Aces Magazine and sent away for: he knows all the lethal blows. There's just one problem: Ceil won't let him stay up after nine o'clock.

"I thought," Ceil says, "a person had to have a whole lot of money to be in the Stock Market. Does Tim have that kind of money?"

Old Tim's Estate

"Not necessarily a whole lot," Hack says, "Estelle mention they think he might been buying on a margin. Way that works, way I understand it, Tim might been buying stocks but only put ten, fifteen percent down on them. Or he might got a loan from his broker. Fellow actually buys and sells the stocks. Then, price the stocks goes up, Tim sells the stocks and pays the balance on the price he bought them for or pays off his loan. Rest is all profit. I'd say Tim had that kind of money. Or then there's Investment Trusts too. Tim might bought stocks in one of them. There's a big one called Shenandoah and one called Blue Ridge. Then the Investment Trust. . . ." But this is as far as Hack can go with the fiduciary strategy involved. All he actually knows about Investment Trusts is a garbled explanation Banty Shanahan, the world's leading authority on many subjects, offered one night at the poolhall. "Anyway, Tim's pretty sharp with a dollar. We know that. My guess, he did pretty well in the Stock Market."

"But how," Bee says, "was Tim buying stock? I thought you had to be in New York in that Stock Market place to do that."

"Not necessarily," Hack says, "he could phone one those brokers I mention. Long distance. In Minneapolis prolly. Buy and sell stocks on the telephone. Or there might be a broker in Winatchee Falls even. One the banks." Banty Shanahan explained all this too, in garbled fashion.

"Well I just hope," Ceil says, "he knew what he was doing. But what do you suppose got into him, or happened to him, he didn't come for supper? Dinner, they call it. Tim always comes home to eat. Or phones Bergda. Where the dickens is he?"

"Prolly just had some car trouble," Hack says, "Some place there's no phone." That's Hack's theory and he'll stick to it. "Buick's a pretty good car. But all them General Motors cars liable to break down you put a few miles on them."

"But all day!" Ceil says, "He could find a phone."

"Or he might went on a business trip," Hack, offering another theory, says.

T.R. St. George

"He'd tell Bergda, he went on a business trip," Ceil says, "Like she said. I tell you, I don't know what to think!"

"Well I just hope he's all right," Bee says. Bee's always been closer to Tim than Ceil was or is. Tim and Ceil, though four years apart with Bee in between, were sibling rivals. There's no rivalry at all in Bee and she really missed Tim when he left home for high school, seldom seen much thereafter but for the summers he spent moaning about his blisters and his sunburn—

"I see something!" Eddie says, "In the ditch!"

Hack brakes the Model T to a slow halt, depresses the reverse pedal, slowly reverses, halts the T and Eddie (ignoring Ceil's order, "Let your dad look!") scrambles out of the Ford and into the ditch. What he saw is a battered abandoned milk can. He and Hack get back in the T and ten minutes later they're home. It's getting onto Bee's bedtime and Saturday's another work day.

They find Ernie Hoff fooling with the Atwater-Kent, listening to static, he has radio privileges when alone in the house. He just got WGN in Chicago, Ernie says, heard the call letters anyway, but that might be his imagination. He also says he spent the evening in Al's Repair Shop helping Al "uphook" the control cables to the rudder and vertical stabilizer on the airplane-under-construction. This news irritates Ceil but she has other more serious things on her mind. Then Ernie says it's his bedtime and goes up to his room. Ernie's an early riser, up every morning at six. Bee, who sleeps on a pullout couch in the parlor off the living room/dining room, sets her wind-up alarm clock for five-thirty and has Ernie's breakfast and Hack's, Hack's another early riser, on the table an hour later.

Hack says he guesses he could use Eddie, Eddie proposes this, to help look in the ditches along the county road on the way to Henry Heaney's farm and Ceil against her better judgment, it's way past ten o'clock, finally lets Eddie join this expedition.

Hack and Eddie drive back to the Precious Blood church on County Road O and down County Road R to Henry Heaney's farm and a bit

Old Tim's Estate

beyond to where the MSP&P tracks cross County R, but see no sign of Timothy J. Heaney or his Buick, then drive home. They do no converse much en route. They seldom do. Eddie's somewhat in awe of Hack and Hack's apparently content to leave Eddie's upbringing to Ceil and Maddy.

Eddie does ask though, when they turn around on County R, the old Forney place in a dark stand of trees a quarter-mile away across a stubbled field, "Dad? Do you think Uncle Tim might been kidnapped? And the kidnappers gonna ask a ransom for him?"

"No," Hack says, "I don't think so. I think he prolly just had some business somewhere and got held up. Or had car trouble. Some place there's no phone. He might be home by now. We'll find out, your mother phones Bergda."

But Timothy J. Heaney is still missing when Ceil phones, collect, and speaks with Estelle, saying only in case some insomniacs are rubbernecking, "We didn't see anything on our way home and neither did Hack, he took that little drive he mentioned." Off the phone, she says, "I guess Bergda's just about beside herself. Worried sick. Estelle said she'll call in the morning if there's any news." Then shoos Eddie off to bed.

Eddie sleeps in his boxer shorts on a cot in the tiny room, once the storage space, at the top of the stairs, its walls plastered with blurry photos of his favorite football teams, Notre Dame and the Land Grant U Gophers, clipped from the Bugle Call, and illustrations clipped from Air Aces Magazine—Spads, Nieuports and Sopwith-Camels shooting hated German Fokkers down in flames. There's also a clipped photo of his current No. 1 hero, Harold (Hoss) Hossman, a large young man (6-2, 210 pounds) from the Mesabi Iron Ore Range, the LGU Gophers fullback and, some sportswriters think, a possible All-American, an honor far exceeding sainthood in Eddie's opinion, with a football tucked in his arm, straight-arming an invisible tackler.

Ceil and Hack are still up. No doubt they're discussing Timothy J.

T.R. St. George

Heaney's sudden mysterious disappearance and Eddie would like to eavesdrop on that discussion but can only hear their voices mumbling, no words, Ceil shut the door at the foot of the stairs. Curled in his cot, he swiftly dispatches several kidnappers with lethal blows and tries to picture Aunt Bergda "beside herself." Two Aunt Bergdas joined at the hip like the Siamese Twins there was a picture of in The Weekly Reader?

2.

Saturday morning. Eddie sleeps until ten o'clock, wakes slowly, then remembers his Uncle Tim Heaney is missing, maybe kidnapped! Or was anyway when he went to bed. He scrambles into his play clothes: bib overalls, denim shirt and his old hightop black Keds with torn toes. The shirt and overalls still smell faintly of smoke and cigarettes. He slips into Ernie Hoff's room, kills this smell (he hopes) with some of Ernie's lethal after-shave and goes downstairs. Eddie no longer wears his Whoopee pants in Stiles. The red elastic waistband on Whoopee pants needs more research and development. Washed once or twice, this waistband loses its elasticity. Sneaking up behind a kid then, grabbing the seat of his Whoopee pants and yanking them down around his knees is considered pretty funny. Hilarious if, often the case, there's nothing between the pullee and his Whoopee pants. Hinty Murphy's an expert at this. Twice within recent memory on soft summer evenings when half the kids in town were fooling around outside the poolhall Hinty yanked Eddie's Whoopee pants down around his knees. Eddie was wearing his boxer shorts so nobody actually saw his pecker. Nevertheless, he'd like to kill Hinty, slowly, or beat him up anyway. But Hinty's older and bigger, a real athlete, good with his fists. He's been punching his little brother Frankie, eight, and other kids for years, training for when he's fourteen and can fight in the Golden Gloves in Winatchee Falls.

Downstairs, Bee's in the kitchen washing the breakfast dishes and

Ceil is on the phone saying, "Yes, yes, I see, yes. What? I can't hear you. There's somebody on the line. Oh, yes, we'll certainly say a prayer."

"They find Uncle Tim yet?" Eddie says.

"No," Bee says, "I guess not. Not yet. Your mother's talking to Estelle now. Don't you worry your mother about that today."

This is an admonition, Don't worry your mother, Eddie hears several times most days and he has to pee. He goes out to the privy (also called the outhouse, also called the backhouse) Old Tim Heaney had built in November 1922, a two-holer bolted to the small barn in which Old Tim kept a horse for awhile and Hack Devlin, the stall removed, garages the Model T. This privy replaced a free-standing structure several unknown Stiles adolescents tipped over in a rite of passage that Halloween.

It's a cool crisp sunny morning, warm for early November, no snow yet, and the privy's comfortable enough. In mid-winter, twenty degrees below zero, frost rimming its holes, trips to the privy require immense fortitude. Ceil and Bee use a slopjar then, which Bee empties in the privy, but males over six years of age unless laid low with a broken leg or some dread disease or they're awful sissies have to use the privy. There's only one house in Stiles with an indoor bathroom, Harry Kelly's. Harry works for the county, he's a clerk in the Auditor's Office, and had a bathroom and a skeptic tank put in when he inherited some money, no kids to spend it on. All the kids in Stiles watched two men from Schneider's Excavating in Winatchee Falls dig a big hole in the Kellys' backyard and a ditch all the the way to their house and lay a pipe in the ditch and fill the hole with gravel and cover it up. The skeptic tank is not in fact a tank, it's just this hole full of gravel, but the grass there is greener than anywhere else in the yard. Eddie always pees in the Kellys' bathroom when Bee takes old Mrs. Kelly (she's got the dropsy, legs like stovepipes, it's hard for her to get around) a pie or something. He peed in the Timothy J. Heaneys' bathroom too, though he really didn't have to, just for the treat that is.

Peeing in the privy, Eddie tries to hit the hole but splatters the seat (no matter, it will dry) then spends several minutes looking at

Old Tim's Estate

the guns in an old Sears & Roebuck catalog serving its last purpose. Eddie wishes he had a gun, preferably a 22-caliber rifle, but Ceil won't hear of it. He has a Lone Star BB gun and that's bad enough, she says. She's afraid he'll put somebody's eye out with his BB, like happened to Petey Bremer when he was eight and his big brother Kermit, playing William Tell, fired his BB gun at an apple on Petey's head but missed. Missed the apple.

Back in the house, Eddie gobbles his breakfast: cornflakes, a cookie Bee baked and a glass of milk. There's been no sign yet nor any word from Timothy J. Heaney, Ceil reports. "Estelle just said there's nothing new. She knew there were rubberneckers on the line. She'll call again, she said, if there's any news. She didn't go into work this morning. She said she's going in this afternoon." Ceil looks grim and worried, she often looks grim and worried. She also says she has a "miserable headache" and tells Eddie, "Don't you say a word to anybody about your Uncle Tim. It's a family matter."

Eddie promises he won't, crossing his heart and hoping to die to seal this promise, gulps the last of his milk, agrees reluctantly to wear his denim jacket so he won't catch cold and heads for the Great Outdoors, escaping Ceil's miserable headache.

He gets his bike (Hack bought it for him used for $5 in Winatchee Falls and fixed it, there was something wrong with the sprocket) and pedals across the vacant lot where Peterson's Store used to be, nothing left of it now except a basement full of weeds and rusty junk, to the center of the universe—where County Road O and County Road S, two ribbons of gravel slicing west-to-east and north-to-south (and vice versa) across the rolling prairie cross. O and S are eighteen-feet wide out in the country with ditches on both sides but O, also Stile's main street, is wider with no ditches where it goes through Stiles so people can park their cars on it next to some beat-up sidewalks. The sidewalk on the south side of main street runs from in front of where Peterson's Store used to be by Frank Pratt's poolhall, Hack Devlin's garage and bubble-top gas pumps (Regular and High Test, though hardly anybody buys High Test), the basement full of junk and weeds where

T.R. St. George

once stood the cheese factory, Al's Repair Shop and Claude Clarke's Store & Post Office. The store is a small brick building once the Stiles State Bank & Trust. The northside sidewalk runs from in front of Lee J. Lilly's Stiles Hotel, by a vacant lot with trees in it called the park, another basement full of junk and weeds (Pat Clarke's Clothing Store, it burned down before Eddie was born) and the Frohoeft Co. lumberyard. The lumberyard's a long building with Ernie Hoff's office in the front, the rest of it just one wall and a roof, full of stacked lumber, nails in kegs, shingles in bundles, tarpaper in rolls, cement in 50-pound paper sacks etc. The Stiles Hotel is a big two-story frame building with flaking paint, two privies in its backyard and two chimneys Hack Devlin calls a "fire-trap waiting to happen." It's not had any overnight guests for years but a dozen or so old-timers, retired farmers and their wives and some dead farmers' widows who have sons working their land and a little money, enough to keep them out of the County Poor Farm, live there. The gasoline generator Lee J. Lilly runs sparingly is beside the privies. The residents have hotplates and cooking privileges and dim electric lights until nine p.m. when Lee J. Lilly shuts the generator off. Then they go to bed. On sunny days and warm summer evenings these old folks sit on chairs on the sidewalk outside the hotel and gab. The old women talk, boast, about their grandchildren and the old men goddamn the goddamn railroads and the goddamn corporations perceived to be screwing honest farmers and the Goddamn Government perceived to be aiding and abetting the goddamn railroads and goddamn corporations. On rainy days and in the winter they gab in the lobby or struggle with jigsaw puzzles. Now and then, one dies.

There are a dozen big old oak trees in the park and an old tire kids can swing on Al Morris hung on a rope from one of them. Those trees, it's thought, were there two-hundred years ago, long before there were any white men except maybe some French fur-traders in the territory. Indians probably camped under them and Hinty Murphy once found what he claims is an arrowhead in the park, but it might just be a stone.

Old Tim's Estate

The grain elevator that didn't burn down, six stories counting its cupola, its red paint faded, looms up beyond the park beside the MSP&P tracks. This elevator's mostly closed except during the harvest season and sneaking into it when it's closed, avoiding the huge spiders that infest it, and climbing the broken ladder in one of its pitch-dark bins, sixty feet straight up, is another thing Eddie's not supposed to do. Ceil's afraid he'll fall and get killed. But Eddie does it anyway. It's a rite of passage for all the prepubescent boys in Stiles and Margie Bremer does it too. The climbers on a clear day, peering through the broken windows in the cupola, can see the top of the stone bell tower on the Precious Blood church a mile to the west.

The broken sidewalks flanking main street date to the days when for a time it was thought Stiles soon would be a bustling little city.

George P. Stiles, a surveyor by trade, was twenty-eight when hired by the Milwaukee St. Paul & Pacific Railroad in 1884. A year later he was named chief surveyor when the former chief surveyor cut his arm on a rusty piece of iron on a MSP&P work train and died of the lockjaw. The MSP&P by then had pushed its Main Line across south central Wisconsin and, following a year's delay while it raised more money, across the Mississippi River on a long iron bridge and up out of the hills beyond the river, its ancient banks in prehistoric times when, according to The Weekly Reader, the last Great Glacier was retreating and the Mississippi was five miles wide.

George P. Stiles was directed to survey a route westward from those hills for the MSP&P's Main Line and locate a logical place at which to divert a Branch Line north to St. Paul. He set off in the Spring of 1886 with his transit etc., three men and a wagon, and followed the ridge lines west, trailed by two MSP&P lawyers in a buggy who where necessary bought the right-of-way George surveyed, though title to much of this land still rested with the federal government and was simply transferred to the MSP&P to encourage and in part finance its push westward. Deep in Winatchee County two years later (George P. Stiles and the lawyers wintered in Milwaukee at the MSP&P's head office,

T.R. St. George

the three men laid off) George P. Stiles found a ridge tending north to Winatchee Falls and beyond and chose that spot for the start of the Branch Line. There already was dirt track there (the Old Dubuque Trail, the stagecoach route between Dubuque, Iowa, and St. Paul) and a ramshackle log tavern and livery stable called Redmond Corners in honor of Old Tom Redmond, the tavern-keeper.

All along the right-of-way he surveyed, George P. Stiles, as was the custom with the railroads then under construction, platted future towns every twelve miles or so, six miles considered an easy half-day trip for farmers with wagons full of corn or grain, or driving livestock, they wished to ship. The lots platted in these future communities, subsequently sold to the gullible, were in fact the MSP&P's principle initial source of income. George P. Stiles also named these plats, choosing in most cases as was the custom the names of MSP&P executives or their offspring, putting them on the map, at least for a time. A good many plats were never developed. Some that were prospered for a few years then died. A few survived and grew. At Redmond Corners, exhibiting some hubris, George P. Stiles named his plat Stiles, putting himself on the map.

The Stiles lots sold well, there being many gullible convinced that what with the Branch Line and all Stiles soon would be a major transportation hub. There were several houses and a competing tavern there in 1890 when wild Irish laborers laid the Main Line tracks through the plat and away to the west and the Branch Line tracks to Winatchee Falls. Freight trains soon rolled over the Main Line and the Branch line, spewing smoke and soot, their long lonely fading whistles in the dead of night a call to far places, romance and adventure. The freights were followed by passenger trains, likewise spewing smoke and soot, three a day each way through Stiles on the Branch Line, five on the Main Line. They all stopped and the eastbound Maine Line trains, enticing the truly adventurous, went all the way to Milwaukee. There still are six trains daily but the Main Line Omaha Flyer doesn't stop anymore.

Old Tim's Estate

By then, Eddie Devlin's heard, here were more than two-hundred people in Stiles. The MSP&P was drilling a well and building the big wooden water tank on thirty-foot legs that still stands beside the Maine Line on Stiles' western edge, and laying the long spur track on which it now parks boxcars, etc. The grain elevator that burned down and the one that's left were under construction and local boosters were confident the population soon would top three-hundred, at which point Stiles would become an "incorporated village" and elect its own mayor and a Village Council. But other railroads, among them the Chicago & Northwestern and Chicago & Great Western, were criss-crossing the prairie with their tracks at the time. Competition for freight and passengers soon grew fierce and early in the Panic of '93 the MSP&P abruptly went bankrupt. Filed for bankruptcy anyway, Chapter 11, which it survived, then struggled on, eventually pushing its Branch Line to St. Paul and its Maine Line to Omaha. It never did reach the Pacific.

The Stiles State Bank & Trust likewise collapsed in '93 and did not recover. It failed, taking many gullible local farmers with it, though Old Tim Heaney, Eddie's heard, was smart enough to have put no trust or money in it. The Panic also slowed the construction underway but for the water tank. The MSP&P spur was not completed until the turn of the century and the elevators, though completed, were often empty. Winatchee Falls' bright lights beckoned some Stiles residents: they mesmerized Young Tim Heaney. Fires as noted sent other residents packing in their aftermath. Smallpox, chickenpox, scarlet fever, diphtheria, pneumonia, other assorted ills, old age, occasional accidents and the 1918-19 Flu Epidemic carried off a good many more. The rosy "incorporated village" dream faded, then was abandoned. The Tilden Township Board (five old codgers thought prone to take bribes when considering bids for township road work, Claude Clarke one of them) still governs Stiles. So to speak. And the population went right on dwindling until stabilizing at its present hundred or so along about 1920, the year Eddie was born.

T.R. St. George

Eddie does two fast laps on his bike on the south-side-of-main-street sidewalk, yanking the front wheel into the air over the bumps, showing off for Margie Bremer and two little kids, Buddy Douglas' sister June and Shirlee Wallace, playing in the park. Margie's hanging by her knees from the old tire, showing all her grimy underpants and her belly-button. Otherwise, downtown Stiles, somnolent under a clear blue sky, appears bereft of human life. There are two dogs, Al Morris' part-airdale and Lenny Gibbons' part-collie, flopped down on the sidewalk in front of the lumberyard, and the Tastee Bread truck's parked outside the poolhall but the driver's inside gabbing with Frank Pratt.

Truth be told, Eddie sometimes thinks, though he's not got much to compare it with except Winatchee Falls, Stiles, most days, is a dreary little place: he's heard Ceil call it that. Just a faint smear of not-very-advanced civilization on the endless rolling prairie. He thinks that now just for a minute while surveying main street's dusty gravel. Stiles' other streets, there are only two, are dirt roads, dusty in the summer, icy in the winter, deep in mud in the spring and fall. An ambitious plan to gravel these streets was abandoned by the Tilden Township Board when all the bids came in two high unaccompanied (it's thought) by suitable bribes. Stiles and its inhabitants are cut off from the rest of the world several times each winter when blizzards howl across the prairie, piling ten-foot drifts on County O and County S and the MSP&P tracks and nobody's car will start anyway, and again for a time each spring when frost boils turn long stretches of O and S into quagmires.

Nevertheless, Stiles is Eddie's faint smear of not-very-advanced civilization and it's a "better" smear, he's sure, this a proposition he'd defend with his life, then any of the other nearby unincorporated communities (Tilden, Judgment, Predmore, Simpson) George P. Stiles platted. It's certainly a better smear than Simpson anyway, six miles to the north on the MSP&P Branch Line, which, though it has a working cheese factory, has but eighty inhabitants. The Simpson Post Office is in somebody's house. Stiles also has or seems to have, another claim to

Old Tim's Estate

fame, more than its share of eccentrics. There's Banty Shanahan for one. Ernie Hoff, some would say, a man who thinks he's building an airplane he'll fly. Willie Bostwick for sure, a grown man, but he had the sleeping sickness when he was a kid and he's feeble-minded now, drools, and is rarely seen: his mother keeps him locked up in their house: she's afraid he'll walk in front of a train or something. Old Tom Ticke. A skinny old man with a scraggly white beard, Old Tom lives with his sister Jessie, an old maid, in their late parents' old house: their parents left them the house and some money. Old Tom, the story goes, was kicked in the head by a horse when twelve, forty years ago, and hasn't said a word since. He communicates, more or less, with grunts and gestures. He does farm work, wasting no time in conversation, chops wood, mostly old fence posts, he sells in the winter, spades gardens in the spring, collects the village trash with his wheelbarrow, a one-man Sanitation Department, paws through this trash for stuff he deems useful, dumps the rest in the village dump, the hole full of ashes where the elevator that burned down used to be. Stiles kids tease Old Tom, he's considered fair game, imitating his grunts and gestures, which he mostly ignores, but are secretly afraid of him.

Banty, Ernie, Willie, Old Tom. Eddie could if asked provide most of Stiles' current Census Data, name but for some infants' given names every resident and all the dogs (cats don't count) along with their ethnic backgrounds and breeds (mostly mixed), locate their places of residence (owned or rented) and cite all the employed adults' type and place of employment, etc. There are, counting the Stiles Hotel and the MSP&P Depot, twenty-two houses—Buddy Douglas' dad is the Depot Agent and the Douglasses live upstairs in the Depot. Counting the Depot and the Post Office, there are ten business ventures: the poolhall, Hack Devlin's garage and gas station, Al's Repair Shop, the Stiles Hotel, the lumberyard, the Midwest Milling Co. elevator that didn't burn down, Claude Clarke's store and Poop Clarke's cream route. There are two farmers, Lenny Gibbons and Alfred Hock: their fields are out in the country but their houses and barns and silos etc. are in Stiles. There's also the District 14 school

T.R. St. George

and the Lutheran church but they're really not businesses ventures and the Lutheran minister, the Rev. Leif Rehnwall, doesn't live in Stiles. He lives in Tilden and comes over Sunday afternoons except if there's a blizzard or frost boils for a service, mainly a sermon that Bunkie Olson, whose parents drag him there, says "You don't think is never ever gonna end!"

Stiles' population counting Miss Mott, the teacher who rooms-and-boards at the Boettchers, consists of sixty-six adults, thirty-six juveniles not yet twenty-one (twenty-two go to school), thirty dogs including Beans, Bee's some-kind-of-terrier (it turned up hungry two years ago and Bee took it in) and four infants, one of which as Eddie vaguely understands it has no last name. Sylvia, the oldest Bremer girl, she's nineteen, produced this infant at home a month ago. It's a boy she calls Bert but she's not married to anybody. This is a mystery never discussed in Eddie's presence at the Devlins but he's heard some older juveniles, Poop Clarke and his pals, discuss it. It seems to evoke in them mild shock and snickers, more snickers than shock, and Hinty Murphy's big brother Bert, he's twenty and drives a Winatchee Moving & Storage truck, seems to be implicated.

But none of this actually interests Eddie much. He doesn't know for sure, no one ever told him and to this point he's seldom wondered much, exactly what the baby business is all about. Bee's theory, which she shared with him and he embraced for awhile, was a stork, a big bird, brought them. But then he saw a picture of a stork in The Weekly Reader, a large ungainly bird in a messy nest somewhere in Holland, and began to wonder where Bee was getting her information—how a stork with a baby in a sling in its beak could fly into anybody's house? Then he heard somewhere that old Mrs. Kelly before she got the dropsy "delivered babies," delivered him in fact, and thought for as time the storks brought Mrs. Kelly the babies, which she then delivered the way Tim Redmond delivers the mail on his Rural Route. Numerous kids, however, Margie Bremer chief among them, scoffed at this theory. Eddie abandoned it and by osmosis, more or less, got and now has a handle, more or less, on the baby business.

Old Tim's Estate

Babies come from their mother's stomach. How they get there is still a mystery though numerous kids younger than he is, Margie Bremer for one, claim to know all about that and seem to find it fascinating. Getting married, Eddie thought, was the first step—but maybe not.

Whatever, his two laps finished, Eddie pauses, straddling his bike, on the sidewalk outside Claude Clarke's store, the former State Bank & Trust building, which stood vacant for some years after the Bank & Trust failed, then was some other business for awhile, which also failed, before Claude Clarke bought it with his cheese factory insurance money and opened his store. The old Bank & Trust vault is still inside it, a massive steel door with a combination dial on it set into the rear wall behind the counter at which Claude when he's the Postmaster sells stamps (two cents for a letter, penny for a postcard) and the racked boxes with little glass doors with numbers on them, everybody in Stiles has one, he puts the mail in. The Devlins and Bee share Number 32. Claude stacks mail two big for the boxes (packages, seed catalogs and the Sears & Roebuck and Montgomery Ward summer and winter catalogs) on the floor behind the counter. Tim Redmond, Old Tom the tavern-keeper's grandson, delivers the mail and catalogs to the farmers and other people who live out in the country on his Rural Route, thirty miles he drives six days a week in his new Model A Ford coupe or in a horse-and-cutter in the winter, driving on the wrong side of the road sometimes so he can reach the mailboxes, but everybody's used to that. Tim's considered a lucky devil, paid by the Government, never misses a pay check, also finds time to farm eighty acres. Claude Clark's a lucky devil too, paid by the Government to be the Postmaster while running his store and with Poop's help the cream route. Claude's generally thought to be the richest man in Stiles, though Frank Pratt and Harry Kelly also are reckoned to be doing pretty well. Claude, the local lore has it, keeps his money locked up in the old Bank & Trust vault.

Eddie does not go into Claude Clarke's store. Claude, a skinny man in his late fifties with a round protruding belly who wears striped shirts and a tie, the tie proving he's a businessman, doesn't like kids in his store. He's mean to kids, thinks they steal, shoos them out unless accompanied by an adult. Eddie rides back to Al's Repair Shop, a frame shed with a wide door Al and his dad, a carpenter, built on the livery stable ruins next-door to the cheese factory ruins. The shop's closed. Al's probably making a house-call, out somewhere with his 1924 Dodge truck and portable welding equipment, fixing a broken farm machine. Still on his bike, Eddie peers through the little window in the door at Ernie Hoff's airplane-under-construction, he'll check it in detail later, then rides on to his dad's garage, its wide door open to the street, where he parks his bike.

Hack Devlin's got the hood up on the Hupmobile he's fixing and his head in the engine, muttering at intervals "goddamn it."

Hack with his head in the Hup.

Old Tim's Estate

Hups are hard to work on, in addition to which this one belongs to Father Callahan, who no doubt will expect a 100 percent clerical discount when it's fixed. Hack switches to "shucks" when Eddie turns up at his elbow, Ceil doesn't like Eddie to hear swearing, and backs out of the Hup.

"They dint find Uncle Tim yet," Eddie reports. "Can I earn some money, Dad?"

Hack puts Eddie to work washing Hupmobile parts in gasoline. Eddie sticks with that for fifteen minutes, the garage a pleasant familiar place with a smell—grease, old oil, gasoline—he likes, but leaves the parts soaking when Tim Redmond, ready to begin his Rural Route, pulls up at Hack's gas pumps to fill his Model A with Regular. Hack goes out to pump the Regular and clean Tim's windshield and Eddie trails along for a good look at the Model A, which he and Hack consider just abut the last word in an automobile for the masses.

Automobiles loom large in Eddie's life and the lives of all the small boys he knows. The automobiles people drive pretty much establish their place in the scheme of things (or are thought to) as firmly as Burke's Peerage sorts out the British aristocracy. Given a glimpse of a hubcap or grill, Eddie and his friends can instantly identify, make and model, every automobile they're likely to see and promptly slot its driver on the socioeconomic scale. There are lots of makes but, not counting trucks, essentially only four models: two-door sedans (coupes), four-door sedans, two-door convertibles and, some makes only, rare four-door convertibles called cabriolets. Eddie's never seen one of those, just a picture of one, a Lincoln, in The Weekly Reader. There also were pictures of a Dusenberg and a Rolls-Royce, the only foreign car anybody ever heard of, but the given truth is only movie stars can can afford those cars. The Rolls-Royce cost fifteen-thousand dollars! The "best car" for anybody except a movie star is generally thought to be a 12-cylinder Pierce-Arrow, but they don't make them any more. Packards, Lincolns, Cadillacs, each with its juvenile adherents, are next best, followed by (most kids think) Buicks, Chryslers and DeSotos. A step down in the peerage, subject to some argument, are Hupmobiles, LaSalles, Oldsmobiles, Pontiacs and, farther down, Studebakers, Dodges and Nashes. Finally, subject to endless sometimes violent debates, are the Big Three in terms of sales: Model A Fords, Chevrolets and Plymouths. The Devlins' Model T Ford, "enclosed" though it be with glass windows that roll up and down (older Ts have detachable side-curtains made of canvas and isinglass), is a "Tin Lizzie," fast becoming a joke. Eddie frequently says a little prayer: "Please, God, help Dad get a new car." He leaves the details to God.

Filled up, Tim Redmond pays for his gas, $1.70 for ten gallons, and drives off in his Model A, mail and Christmas catalogs piled high on the front seat. Hack goes back to work on the Hupmobile and Eddie starts fishing for the parts he left soaking, but another exciting event (by local standards) puts an end to that. Slicky Riordan and Whip Rahilly roar up on Slicky's new Harley-Davidson motorcycle, Whip on the buddy seat, and skid to a stop at the garage door. Whip asks Hack if he can use some tools, tighten the chain on the Harley? Hack says sure. Whip wheels the Harley into the garage, gets the tools he needs from Hack's cluttered workbench and starts work on the chain while Slicky, wearing a leather jacket, stands at the door smoking a tailor-made cigarette. Eddie promptly abandons the Hupmobile parts and edges close to the Harley, admiring its chrome and the 100 mph on its speedometer.

Whip Rahilly and Eddie are some kind of cousins, Old Ed Devlin's sister Julia married Old John Patrick Rahilly years ago, but Whip's older, big for his age, sixteen like Slicky, and usually as now pretty much ignores Eddie. So does Slicky, busy blowing smoke rings. Whip's real name naturally is John Patrick, but he was a wild little kid, started climbing his dad's windmill, sixty feet straight up, when he was six, fell from it half way up a year later, breaking his arm, but went right on climbing it, cast and all. "That kid's a whip," his Granny Rahilly said at the time and "Whip" he's been ever since. Slicky Riordan, a short fat adolescent, his real name's Sean Leonard Jr., also comes honestly by his nickname: his thick black hair's slicked flat with some

Old Tim's Estate

kind of hair oil. Whip and Slicky are farm kids, they live on big adjoining farms at the far north edge of the Precious Blood Parish, but Slicky's dad, Sean Leonard Sr., doesn't farm, somebody else works his land on shares. Sean Leonard Sr. owns a feed mill and a feed business and scattered real estate, mostly commercial, in Winatchee Falls. He's another rich man, the Harley he gave Slicky for his sixteenth birthday proof of that. Whip helps his dad farm but he'd a lot rather tinker with machinery, preferably automobiles. Whip's got a serious love affair going with the internal combustion engine. He helps Hack Devlin in Hack's garage every chance he gets, not paid, just happy like Hack used to be to crawl around under automobiles, explore their parts, bang his head and skin his knuckles and get his hands greasy taking them apart and putting them back together again.

"Can I sit on it?" Eddie, meaning the Harley, says.

"No," Slicky, blowing another smoke ring, says. He's mean to kids like Claude Clarke.

Whip tightens the chain, thanks Hack for the use of the tools, wheels the Harley out of the garage and, along with Slicky, straddles it, Eddie watching all this with great envy. Slicky kicks the starter, twists the throttle, producing an almighty noise, pops the clutch and tears up main street, Whip clinging tight to Slicky's torso, as far as Claude Clarke's store, where he whips the Harley through a sliding 180-degree turn, flinging loose gravel, scaring old Mrs. Gibbons in her wheelchair on her porch across the street half out of her wits, then roars back down main street and away to west on County Road O, trailing a cloud of dust.

Eddie goes back to washing Hupmobile parts. He'd give just about anything to own a Harley Davidson motorcycle and do 180s in the middle of main street, scaring old Mrs. Gibbons. But Ceil, of course, afraid he'll get killed, will never let him have one. He'll have to wait until he's twenty-one, a time so distant he scarcely can imagine it. Hack's got his head back in Father Callahan's Hupmobile, skinning his knuckles and swearing under his breath.

T.R. St. George

More time passes, then Buddy Douglas turns up on the new bike he got for his birthday, a bike with balloon tires and red reflectors on the fenders, front and back, half of which his dad, a stingy Scotchman, says is Buddy's Christmas present. Buddy parks his bike at the door and comes into the garage. "Jeepers," he says, "I just seen that Slicky Riordan and another guy on Slicky's motorcycle. They must been goin' like a hunnert miles an hour!"

"Yeah, Slicky and my cousin, Whip Rahilly," Eddie says, "They was just in here, fix the chain on it. It'll go a hunnert. I seen the speedometer." Buddy no doubt is sorry he missed that (he too would give just about anything to own a motorcycle) but doesn't say anything. Buddy's a tall skinny kid with red hair and freckles who never says a whole lot.

Eddie tells Hack he's washed all the parts and asks, Can him and Buddy play with some the tools? No, Hack says, tools aren't toys, they cost money, and gives Eddie a dime, pretty good pay all things considered. Eddie and Buddy go next door to the poolhall, where Frank Pratt is putting ice the Tastee Bread delivered in his cooler. Eddie, a big spender, buys two grape pops Frank lifts from the cooler. They drink this pop slowly, making it last, it's ice-cold and delicious, sitting on the broken chairs on the sidewalk in front of the poolhall, now and then observing Margie Bremer's grimy underpants while she swings upside down from the old tire in the park.

Eddie's bursting to tell Buddy, tell somebody, his Uncle Tim Heaney is missing, probably kidnapped, but promised Ceil he wouldn't, crossed his heart and hoped to die in fact. But he didn't promise he wouldn't rescue Uncle Tim. "Hey, Buddy." he says, "whyn't we ride our bikes out the old Forney place this afternoon? We ain't been there in awhile." They can reconnoiter the old Forney place, sneaking through the trees and underbrush that surround it, looking for signs of kidnappers.

"Yeah, okay, I guess," Buddy says, "There ain't nuthin' else to do. Let's take out BB guns, shoot some pigeons or something, we see any."

Old Tim's Estate

"Yeah, we might see some pigeons. Okay, I'll come over your house after dinner and we'll take off." The BBs are a good idea. Best be armed, though of course they're both skilled in Judo, know all the lethal blows.

"What the the heck you doin' anyway?" Buddy Douglas , standing amid the tall weeds and overgrown lilac bushes behind the old Forney house, a weather-beaten old wreck with all its windows broken, says. "Crawlin' around on your belly?"

"Just lookin'," Eddie says, "see there's anybody here." He's squirming through the lilacs, his BB at the ready.

"There ain't ever nobody here," Buddy says, "There ain't nobody lives here. You know that. C'mon, less go inside, see there's any pigeons."

They reached the old Forney place ten minutes ago, puffing along on their bikes from Stiles to the Precious Blood church and down County Road R past Henry Heaney's place, waving to Henry, bent over some kind of farm machine in his yard, thirty minutes in the saddle, then pushed their bikes across the stubbled field between County R and the old Forney place, somebody else works that land now, parked their bikes at the edge of the trees that surround the old place and at Eddie's insistence, Buddy humoring him, slipped cautiously through the trees to their present position behind the old house, where Eddie started squirming through the weeds and the lilacs, searching for car tracks or other signs of kidnappers but finding none, not a thing.

Buddy's had enough of caution. He barges through the grass growing wild in the yard and across the sagging porch and goes into the house, the backdoor's missing, and Eddie, rising, follows him. The kidnappers probably have Uncle Tim bound-and-gagged-tied-hand-and-foot somewhere else but the old Forney place was worth a try.

They've been inside the old Forney house before and so have other kids. There's poop on the living room floor. It's a filthy old house, bare of furniture, the Forneys on departing for parts unknown after a farm machine chopped one of Purvis Forney's legs off and the First National Bank of Winatchee Falls foreclosed on their mortgage took everything they owned with them. The roof leaks, rain's stained all the wallpaper, which is peeling, and it's full of mice, but it's a good place to play except it's so smelly. Sometimes it's a castle, more often it's a Western saloon, a hangout for gunfighters. Buddy fires his BB at a mouse scuttling along a baseboard but misses. There are no pigeons. They poke around for awhile and find an empty whiskey bottle and a torn shoe in an upstairs bedroom. Hobos waiting for an MSP&P freight slowed by the long grade on the Main Line a hundred yards away sometimes hole-up in the old Forney house.

They leave the house and explore the old barn on the place. It's half collapsed, the roof falling in, full of wasps, but there aren't any pigeons there either. They balance the whiskey bottle on a fence post and take turns shooting at it with their BBs until Buddy finally breaks it.

But this adventure soon palls. They get their bikes, push them across the field and ride back to Henry Heaney's place, where Eddie's Aunt-by-marriage Emma gives them cookies and milk. Henry's still out in the yard, swearing at his farm machine. Emma says their son, Little Tim, six, is doing his chores, picking up eggs, farm kids always have chores to do, and his baby sister's asleep but they can look at her if they want to. Eddie and Buddy decline this treat, who wants to look at a baby? Eddie would like to talk to Henry, sound him out about Uncle Tim's mysterious disappearance, assuming Henry's heard about that, though Henry's never very talkative. But Buddy, terminally bashful in Emma's presence, sticks to Eddie like glue, scuttling any chance to discuss this family matter, and, done with the cookies, they get back on their bikes and depart.

They're taking a little break, standing beside their bikes after puffing up the hill between the Precious Blood church and Stiles, when Buddy says, "What was the big idea you wanna sneak up onna old Forney place? There ain't never nobody there."

It's a family matter but Eddie can't keep it a family secret any longer. How many kids ever had a secret like it and what good's a secret if nobody else knows it? He's cautious though. "First you got to promise, Buddy. Cross your heart and hope to die I never told you.

Old Tim's Estate

My mother kill me, she ever finds out I told you." Buddy complies with this demand. "My Uncle Tim lives in Winatchee Falls was kidnapped! We're pretty sure he was anyway. He's pretty darn rich and the kidnappers, they prolly got him hid and tied up some place while they waitin' for their ransom. I thought they might took him the the old Forney place. That's what they do, y'know, crimnulls kidnap somebody. They take them some place they can hide them good while they waitin' for their ransom—"

"How you know," Buddy, a skeptic, says, "he was kidnap?"

"Well he just disappear! Yesterday. He went to his office like he always does but he never got there, girl works his office said. He never come home for his supper either—dinner, they call it. And like I told you, he's pretty darn rich. He sells insurance. He was in the Stock Market. He just bought a new Buick four-door. Well, last June. It's got wire wheels and white sidewalls tires and his 'nitials on it. Onna front doors. What they call momograms. He gets them painted on."

Buddy's reaction is disappointing. "Yeah, well, he might been kidnap, I guess, he's rich like you say. How much ransom the kidnappers want?"

"They ain't ask yet, I don't think. Or they might by now. Or they might be torchering him, y'know, find out how much money's he's got."

"You ever read that story, Ransom the Red Chief? Kidnappers pretty sorry they ever kidnap that kid, time it was over."

"Yeah, I read it. I mean my mother read it me. I wouldn't paid no ransom for that lousy kid either. But cripes, Buddy, that's just a story! You ever have an uncle was kidnapped?"

"I don't know. I might of." But Buddy no doubt is suppressing some envy: both his uncles are MSP&P brakemen, neither worth kidnapping. "C'mon, we better get home."

They mount their bikes and pedal in silence the rest of the way to Stiles, where they split up. Buddy goes home and Eddie pedals on to Al's Repair Shop for a look at Ernie Hoff's airplane-under-construction, something he does most days. He's half sorry now he told Buddy his Uncle Tim was kidnapped. What does Buddy care? But Eddie's reasonably sure, sincerely hopes anyway, Buddy won't tell anybody else. Buddy after all crossed his heart and hoped to die—though that's scarcely an infallible guarantee.

Al's Repair Shop is open. The airplane-under-construction occupies half of it. The fuselage, twenty-feet long, set on bicycle wheels, is a frame made of one-by-one ash braces Al turned out on his wood lathe and screwed and glued together and covered with thin canvas stretched tight, which Ernie recently shellacked. The airplane is or will be a two-seat biplane, the forward seat just to ride in, $5 for a ten-minute ride in Ernie's calculations. Ernie once let Eddie look at the blueprints with the understanding Eddie wouldn't touch them. Ernie the pilot will sit in the rear seat. That one has a rudimentary wooden dashboard with holes cut into it for the ignition switch and some instruments, a joystick and rudder pedals and the wires connecting those to the tail planes are "up-hooked" like Ernie said. The wings, thirty-feet-by-four, flat on the bottom, slightly curved on top, likewise ash frames covered with thin canvas stretched taught and lightly shellacked, rest against one wall. They'll be joined to the fuselage, there's not enough in the shop for this, once the engine's installed and the fuselage is rolled across the street to the lumberyard. The ten-gallon gas tank Hack Devlin salvaged from a '21 Nash beyond repair and metal engine mounts are in place at the front end of the fuselage, that part not covered with canvas so the engine (the four-cylinder T Hack's tuning up) can be got at for overhauls and repairs. Hack's also fitting this engine with a new drive shaft that will spin the propeller. Al made the propeller, four big oak blades six feet long he turned out on his lathe and bolted to a metal collar he salvaged from a broken farm machine. It's leaned up against the shop wall beside with the wings.

Al and Hack and Ernie have been working on the airplane in their spare time since mid-June, though Ernie's principal contribution, besides the shellacking, was a lot of bad advice. He also bought the material, of course. Ernie's tight with a dollar but he has a dream.

Old Tim's Estate

He's paid Al and Hack $15 each on account for their labor and told them, keep track of their time. He'll pay them in full once he "der stormbarning starts and der loop-der-loop looping at County Fairs and people rides giving," and the money's in rolling.

"That'll be the day," Ceil Devlin often says, "He'll break his silly neck!" Ceil also frequently tells Hack, "You'll never see the money he owes you and neither will Al." But Hack and Al really don't care that much about the money. It's been a real challenge, building an airplane, and they're not actually out any money, just their time.

All this began "the day the freight hit Lenny Gibbons' cow and the airplane came." That's the way anyway local historians now describe by far the most exciting day in the annals of Stiles since Peterson's Store burned down and other major local events, births and deaths etc., are now located in time as having happened before or after "the day the freight hit Lenny's cow and the airplane came."

The day was a Saturday late in May, just about the second anniversary of Charles Lindbergh's historic nonstop New York-to-Paris flight. The cow, a Holstein well past her prime taken with wanderlust, pushed through the broken gate in Lenny's sloping pasture beyond the MSP&P tracks and was standing on the Main Line track at high noon, chewing her cud, when a westbound freight came highballing into Stiles at twenty miles an hour. The engineer aboard blew his whistle, three loud piercing blasts that roused half the village but did not startle the old heifer, dumped sand and hit his air-brakes, but all this too late. The cowcatcher on the Baldwin 505 locomotive caught the cow amidships and the freight, air-brakes hissing, wheels screeching, rolled another hundred yards before grinding to a stop behind the park.

MSP&P freights had of course hit other cows, a few horses and a buggy or two over the years and the railroad rule was the train must stop and the engineer or conductor aboard, assuming no loss of human life was involved, settle then and there with the owner of the deceased livestock, presenting this owner with a voucher (not to

T. R. St. George

exceed $25 for a cow) good at any bank on the MSP&P system, thus fore-stalling any subsequent litigation, because juries largely composed of retired farmers still harboring grudges having to do with larcenous freight rates liked to stick it to the railroads.

But Lenny Gibbons—alerted by Ernie Hoff, who saw the cow hit while stacking shingles at the rear of the lumberyard—would have none of that. Leaving his lunch half eaten Lenny charged from his house, met the engineer halfway along the freight and promptly claimed the dead cow was the best one he had, gave the most milk, high in butterfat, produced sturdy calves, etc. By then all the kids in Stiles five and older, Eddie among them, a few younger and a number of adults (Ernie, Frank Pratt, Al Morris, Banty Shanahan, Hack Devlin, half a dozen Stiles Hotel residents) were observing with awe the awful mess (hamburger, blood, hide, bones, guts and cow shit splattered along the tracks) a six-hundred-pound Holstein hit by a train makes. And Lenny and the engineer were still arguing, Lenny holding out for $40, the engineer constrained to $25, when the airplane, a rare phenomenon in Stiles' geographic backwater, appeared low in the southern sky. The cow's splattered remains were promptly forgotten. Everybody, including Lenny and the engineer, turned to watch the airplane.

It was some kind of biplane and its engine was sputtering. It circled once over Stiles, losing altitude, the engine smoking, all eyes upon it, Lenny and his dead cow and the engineer forgotten, lost more altitude, flew low over the village, the engine popping, barely cleared the steeple on the Lutheran Church, almost hit the elevator that didn't burn down and landed, bouncing once or twice, in Lenny's sloping pasture beyond the MSP&P tracks. Lenny's thirty-odd surviving Holsteins, down by the barn at the foot of the slope, promptly panicked and stampeded, Lenny's fierce mad bull lowered his head and pawed the ground, ready to defend his harem against the biggest dragonfly he'd ever seen, and the crowd along the tracks and the freight's four-man crew crawled through and under the freight, Ernie

Old Tim's Estate

Hoff leading the way, and through and over Lenny's sagging pasture fence in a mad rush to reach the pasture and the airplane.

The pilot—a skinny young fellow who needed a shave, wearing a leather jacket and a leather helmet and goggles pushed up on the helmet, a dashing figure straight out of Air Aces Magazine—climbed from the airplane's open cockpit and dropped to the ground. He was on his way to St. Paul, he said, "For the Air Show. Then the goddamn engine give out on me. Goddamn plugs prolly dirty. And my pardner, he's up in St. Paul awready, he's got the goddamn tools. I wunner there's anybody here got any tools? Gimme a hand?"

Hack and Al, naturally, promptly volunteered their services and went to get some tools. By the time they got back around sixty percent of Stiles' ambulatory population, a half dozen farmers and their wives and kids who happened to be buying groceries at Claude Clarke's store and old Mrs. Gibbons, propelled along in her wheelchair and bumped over the MSP&P tracks behind the freight by her daughter Luverne were standing around in the pasture (or sitting in old Mrs. Gibbons' case) gawking at the airplane and the pilot like they were Things From Outer Space.

Hack and Al returned with tools and along with the pilot pulled the spark plugs on the rotary engine, there were nine, and Hack and Al cleaned them, adjusted them for a better spark and replaced them while the pilot spoke briefly with Ernie Hoff then conversed with the crowd, Eddie and the other kids and most of the adults, mouths agape, hanging on his every word. "This a Curtis-Wright aircraft," the pilot said, "It's a pretty good aircraft. And that there's a Curtis-Wright engine. It's a pretty good engine, most the time." He also said everybody should come to the Air Show up in St. Paul to watch him loop-the-loop, perform other acrobatics and stage a mock dogfight with his partner. "And we got a gal wing-walks too," he said, "without no parachute, she scare the bejezzuz out ya." Then he helped Hack and Al gather up their tools.

Willing hands directed by the pilot and Ernie Hoff picked the airplane up by its tail, hauled it up the slope in the pasture and put the tail down close to the broken gate. The pilot told everybody, "Stand clear!" and climbed into the airplane. Banty Shanahan, who claimed to have had experience in this line in France during the Big War, twisted the propeller. The pilot yelled "Contact!" just like the pilots in Air Aces Magazine. Banty heaved on the propeller. The engine fired, sputtered and settled into a steady roar. Lenny's fierce mad bull, down by the barn at the foot of the slope defending his harem, pawed the ground and snorted but decided to hold his peace. The pilot pulled his goggles down, ran the engine up while willing hands held the tail, then yelled, "Let 'er go!" The willing hands let 'er go. The airplane bounced down the sloping pasture halfway to the barn, its wheels churning through fresh cowpies, the fierce mad bull holding his ground, and lifted off. It rose, cleared the barn though barely, circled once low over the crowd, the pilot waving—Lenny's cows and fierce mad bull stampeding again, the bull finally losing his nerve—then climbed into the northern sky. All present stood and watched it until the tiny black dot it became finally vanished. That was when Hack Devlin discovered a pretty good $20 set of his socket wrenches were gone with it, but he's never told Ceil that.

The MSP&P crew got back on the freight. The engineer gave Lenny Gibbons a form to fill out, a claim for one smashed cow valued at $40, warning Lenny it would take the MSP&P a "long time" to process this form, climbed into his locomotive and blew its whistle. The freight chugged away to the west on the Main Line and Lenny went looking for old Tom Ticke to clean up the mess on the tracks.

Hours later at supper at the Devlins, Ernie Hoff, he wasn't his usual phlegmatic self, outlined his dream. "You know vot dot fella der airplane fly tell me?" Ernie said, awed. "He is make fifty dollar a day der airplane flying! County Fairs and Air Shows and stormbarning and people rides giving. Fifty dollar a day! I tink by golly I am a airplane buy and to fly learn and dat do! Der stormbarning go and den loop-the-loop looping and rides giving and rich get!"

Ernie grew up in New Potsdam, a Teutonic enclave sixty miles to

Old Tim's Estate

the west, spoke low Deutsch at home and English, more or less, in school, but did not get a grip on English syntax. No matter, the sum he mentioned was clear enough.

"Fifty dollars a day!" Eddie Devlin had a hard time going to sleep that night, tossing and turning, that monster sum dancing in his brain while he considered a career in aviation, thought by some to be the coming thing since Lindbergh flew his airplane all the way across the Atlantic Ocean. And wing-walkers, Eddie surmised, must be well-paid too, and safe enough if a girl can do it—without a parachute! He can practice on the roof on the chicken coop. Bee was afraid Eddie had a stomach ache or was having a bad dream, all that tossing and turning, but Ceil said, "No, I think he just had too much excitement for one day."

Ernie tossed and turned too, Eddie heard the springs on his bed squeaking, fifty dollars a day! and a future in aviation dancing in his brain.

Ernie's dream, however, soon ran aground on hard economic facts. There are ads for used airplanes in Air Aces Magazine, but the cheapest one Ernie could find was priced at $400, another figure like the National Debt. Then he found the Build Your Own Biplane ad, revised his dream and sent away for the blueprints. Ernie's filled three ten-cent notebooks with calculations and figures he can build the airplane-under-construction for $300, much of that on account until der stormbarning and loop-der-loop looping and rides at county fair giving he starts and the money in rolling is.

Eddie studies the airplane-under-construction. Al's got his head in his metal mask, busy welding something on a farm machine, the blue flame dancing at the end of his acetylene torch too bright to look or he'll go blind or so Eddie's been warned. Eddie looks at it anyway, does not instantly go blind, chalks up another case of erroneous information supplied by adults and studies the airplane further. Eddie's got a dream now too. Someday, he'll learn to fly an airplane, a real fighter airplane like the ones in Air Aces Magazine and should the opportunity arise no doubt shoot numerous hated German Fokkers down in flames. Al, done with his welding, turns off his torch and pulls off his mask.

"Can I sit in the airplane a minute?" Eddie says.

"No," Al says. Al's an only child like Eddie: they're the only ones in Stiles. Well, Al had a sister but she died of the meningitis or something when she was two, before Al was born, so she really doesn't count. Al's never indicated, however, that this shared peculiarity bonds him with Eddie in any way. He probably wouldn't even let Eddie get close to the airplane except Hack's helping build it.

So Al will be sorry when Aces Devlin, an ace three times over, sixteen black crosses on his airplane, comes home to Stiles in his airplane wearing a leather jacket and a white silk scarf and goggles pushed up on his leather flying helmet like the pilots in Air Aces Magazine. Aces Devlin will land his airplane right in the middle of main street so everybody can get a good look at it and it won't look anything like Ernie's airplane, which is going to look like a big box kite. Aces Devlin's airplane will be a lean lethal-looking craft armed with six deadly sinkernized machine-guns like the Airplane-of-the-Future there was a picture of in The Weekly Reader.

Aces Devlin leaves Al's shop, does a lap-and-half on his bike on the sidewalk while dropping several hated Fokkers in flames and finds one-eyed Petey Bremer and his big brother Kermit everybody calls Kerm chalking pictures on the sidewalk in front of where Peterson's store used to be. Petey actually has both his eyes but the right one is sort of white and mushy-looking and he can't see anything with it. The pictures are ovals with pointy ends surrounded by squiggly marks.

"You know what them are?" Kerm says.

"No," Eddie says, "What?"

"Cunts," Kerm says, "What girls got instead peckers. You ever seen one?"

"Sure," Eddie says. In fact, Margie Bremer, they were playing in an empty boxcar, Margie runs boxcars as well as any boy, showed him her

Old Tim's Estate

Thing one drizzly Saturday afternoon a month ago, with the understanding he'd show her his, which he did. Her Thing didn't amount to much, just a little pink slit between her legs when she pulled her underpants down, nothing squiggly, no hair, around it. Neither, apparently, did Eddie's. Margie only said his was "awful little," nowhere near as big as Bert Murphy's when she peeked and saw Bert sticking his in her sister Sylvia standing up in the Bremers' kitchen one Saturday night during the January thaw when her ma and pa were in Winatchee Falls and Kerm and Petey were asleep and Bert and Sylvia thought she was.

Eddie's not done that again, though Margie's twice suggested they do it. He's pretty sure it's something else Ceil would forbid and also, most likely, a springboard for the deadly Unclean Thoughts that Young Bernie Griffin who's studying to be a priest (he's far enough along he gets to wear a long back cassock) and teaches the Catechism class summers in the church basement at Precious Blood says you'll go Straight to Hell for if you have them and don't make "a determined effort," getting down on your knees and praying even, "to put from your mind." Eddie's not told anybody he did that with Margie and he certainly won't tell Kermit Bremer, who beats up on kids who say his sister Margie's dirty.

Eddie wheels off on his bike, leaving the Bremers to their art work, does another lap-and-half on the sidewalk and stops at his dad's garage. Hack Devlin's still got his head in the Hupmobile, muttering "goddamn it" at intervals, taking the Lord's name in vain, also risking Hell or so Young Bernie Griffin often tells the Catechism class, though Eddie's beginning to doubt that. Much of the information supplied by adults seems to be dead wrong.

Some of this information, though, Eddie truly believes. One thing he truly believes is that the population of the world is divided into two unequal groups: those who are Irish, much the smaller of the two, and all the rest, who if they have any sense wish they were Irish. He also believes in Heaven, Hell and Purgatory.

T.R. St. George

Young Bernie Griffin.

    Young Bernie Griffin often describes these After Life locations, Hell with particular relish, just as if he'd been a tourist there. Eddie also believes, he has Young Bernie Griffin's word for it, Heaven is reserved for "practicing Catholics." Practicing until they're perfect, this seems to mean. All the different kinds of Protestants, all the long hours they spend in their churches wasted, and everybody else with a strange religion or no religion at all are all going Straight

Old Tim's Estate

to Hell, eventually. Eddie sometimes thinks this is not exactly "fair." But that's the way it is, apparently. And some practicing Catholics, not yet perfect, are likely to be delayed en route to Heaven and spend years and years in Purgatory, which is more like Hell than a summer camp, Young Bernie Griffin says. Mean Claude Clarke for one, Eddie likes to think, and should that time come he'll leave Claude out of his prayers for "the poor souls in Purgatory" Father Callahan and Young Bernie are always urging people say. There's also a place called Limbo, which is where babies who die before they're baptized go, but Young Bernie's never bothered much with Limbo's accommodations. He'd rather describe Hell.

Babies who die right after they're baptized, still too little to commit any sins, go straight to Heaven and old Mrs. Kelly before she got the dropsy and was still delivering babies fixed it so a few who were just about dead when she delivered them did. Or so Bee, calling old Mrs. Kelly "a saint," once told Eddie. Old Mrs. Kelly dribbled water on their little heads, made the Sign of the Cross, said the magic words and baptized them herself, Joseph if they were boys, Mary if they were girls. Which anybody can do, Bee explained, in those circumstances. Most of these babies were born Catholic but a few were Protestants. Whether in fact old Mrs. Kelly managed to sneak those little Protestants into Heaven is not known, but Bee figures it was worth a try.

All this set Eddie to thinking and a week or so later, never mind the circumstances, when he and Buddy Douglas were fooling around near the pail of water Hack Devlin keeps beside his gas pumps to fill radiators with, Eddie splashed a little water on Buddy, made a discreet Sign of the Cross, like he was batting at a fly, muttered the magic words ("Name the Father the Son 'n the Holy Ghost") and baptized Buddy Buddy. Buddy, unfortunately, recoiled, squealed, "Hey! Jeepers, you gettin' me all wet!" and splashed water on Eddie, which might have started a water fight except Hack yelled from the garage, Leave that water alone! Whether this baptism "took" is of course unclear and will be until Buddy dies and goes to—well, where ever he goes.

T. R. St. George

Still, Eddie thinks, it was worth a try, the least he could do for his best friend: give him a shot at Heaven.

Eddie of course cannot imagine himself or Buddy old or dead at some distant future date (or picture any adult he knows as a child) and finds much of what Young Bernie Griffin has to say mysterious. Adam and Eve, for instance. They're a real puzzle. The first people—a not-very-bright-looking white couple probably around thirty years old, bare naked except for some leaves in the picture Young Bernie showed the Catechism class, which triggered some giggles Young Bernie promptly quelled—Adam and Eve lived for awhile in a place called the Garden of Eden. But then they listened to a snake (a snake that talked?) and did a bad thing: they ate an apple and God threw them out of the Garden of Eden. They must, Eddie surmises, swiped the apple, that's the only logical conclusion. Not much of a crime as crimes go. All the kids in Stiles swipe apples every fall from old Clarence Kunkel's big orchard behind his house next door to the Boettchers. But so it goes. Or so it went for Adam and Eve anyway. Served them right too, they were evicted, Young Bernie Griffin says with relish.

Adam and Eve. They're everybody's great-great-great-great-great-about-a-thousand-times-over-grandparents, which Eddie initially found difficult to believe, what with four-billion people in the world according to The Weekly Reader. But then he thought about the Murphys and the multiplication tables. There are eight Murphy kids. If they all get married and have eight kids (and Bert the way it sounds is already started on that) and those kids get married and have eight kids and those kids get married and have eight kids—well, no time at all there be thousands and thousands of Murphys or half-Murphys or quarter-Murphys. So this is possible. The mystery is that an awful lot of white Adam's and white Eve's descendants, millions and millions of them, turned out to be black or brown or yellow and a few are, or were, Redskins, and almost all of them are heathens, keeping the missionaries busy. Some of them, too, early on, must have married their brothers or sisters or cousins, but Young Bernie's not got into that.

Old Tim's Estate

A mystery all right and Eddie for a time thought he might ask Young Bernie Griffin to explain it, but Young Bernie does not take kindly to questions, especially those he can't answer. His parents are said to be really proud of Young Bernie, especially his mother—he's every Irish mother's dream, a son who's a priest or studying to be one anyway—but some ways he's kind of dumb. Catholics of course have a lot of mysteries to contend with. Fifteen, for instance, that go with the Rosary, though nobody Eddie knows knows all of those except probably Father Callahan and Young Bernie Griffin. The thing to do with all these mysteries, Young Bernie says when some smartass kid asks him a question he can't answer is not to think about them too much but "simply accept them as a Matter of Faith."

Eddie's adopted this rationale. He spends little time, about a minute a month maybe, sorting out these many mysteries. He spends more time though not a whole lot, has been for a year or so, trying to get a handle on Life and What It Means, his Life and Life in general, and wondering what he'll be and do when he grows up, how he'll make a lot of money, etc. But many things of more immediate concern and importance supersede these ruminations. Learning to ride his bike with "no hands." Keeping track of the Major League pennant races and the Land Grant U Gophers' football prowess. Building up his muscles, struggling with pull-ups and push-ups so he'll look like Charles Atlas instead of the miserable "87-pound weakling" in the Charles Atlas Exercise Machine ads in Air Aces Magazine—a wonderful machine, "Satisfaction Guaranteed or Your Money Back," and it comes with an Instruction Manual. But it costs $12.95, another figure like the National Debt.

Eddie props his bike at the door and goes into the poolhall, where Banty Shanahan is telling Frank Pratt, two farmers nursing near beers and Lee J. Lilly how to tell good French champagne from the "cheap stuff"—though it's unlikely this is expertise his listeners will ever need.

Banty's a skinny little man, wouldn't weigh a hundred-and-thirty

T.R. St. George

pounds soaking wet, with it's often said has a big mouth. He was in France for six months in The Big War but got gassed and then shell-shcked and the Army sent him home. He gets a Veteran's Pension, digs the graves in the Precious Blood Cemetery and elsewhere, usually meets the three p.m. Branch Line passenger train every day but Sunday to get the mail and the Bugle Call newspapers and deliver both to the Post Office and does other odd jobs when he feels like it. He lives alone in a tiny house near the MSP&P water tank beside the Main Line tracks his mother, Biddy Shanahan, left him when she died. She died while Banty was in France, found three days later. Banty, Eddie's heard, like the infant Sylvia Bremer calls Bert, did not have a last name when he was born, Biddy then close to forty. Biddy wasn't from Stiles though, so some of this history is cloudy. She was from Hayfield, a village George P. Stiles platted on the Main Line twenty-four miles west of Stiles and named for an MSP&P vice-president, Bertram Hayfield, which, just why a mystery, proved a minor boomtown: around twevce-hundred people live there now. But Biddy, so the story goes, couldn't live there after Banty was born at the turn of the century, so Banty's father, whoever he was, a gentleman up to a point, bought Biddy the little house near the water tank with an outdoor privy behind it before he vanished from her life. Gave her some money too, many think. Biddy, her story also goes, was working just prior to all this, she was a secretary, for Mr. Hawley Bush, a skinny little Hayfield lawyer and Republican State Senator who, Eddie's heard it said at the poolhall, most likely was "the nigger in the woodpile." Whatever that means. The poolhall regulars cite the fact Banty's got a big mouth, never shuts up, as proof there likely was a lawyer and/or a politician in his family tree. That's the way lawyers and politicians make a living, the regulars say: talk talk talk.

 In fact, this a recent report from Lenny Gibbons, an MSP&P lawyer will be coming to Stiles next week, finally, to talk talk talk with Lenny and, this lawyer said he "trusts" in the letter he wrote Lenny, "reach a mutually satisfactory financial settlement as regards" the old Holstein the freight killed the day the airplane came. Lenny's still

74

Old Tim's Estate

holding out for $40 and with Claude Clarke's help wrote the MSP&P's Head Office in Milwaukee several angry marginally literate letters citing that figure.

Biddy when first she came to Stiles and her sad story got out was, naturally, Eddie's also heard, pretty much ostracized by all the local Good Christians, though Biddy didn't seem to mind that much. She subsequently cleaned house for Mrs. Kelly and the Claude Clarkes, took care of old Mrs. Gibbons when Luverne when off to the Winona Teachers College, an experiment that failed, then got a permanent job keeping the books at Lee J. Lilly's Stiles Hotel. Somehow, Biddy survived, and so did Banty, who though small was obnoxious, with a big mouth, and had a lot of fights while a kid and an adolescent, losing most of them. And Biddy, as the saying goes, earning reluctant blessings, "raised Banty Catholic" though "fallen away" herself. She got him rides Sundays to the ten o'clock mass at Precious Blood: the Good Christians could scarcely refuse to perform that Good Work. Banty made his First Communion and his Confirmation and still goes to mass most Sundays and makes his Easter Duty: Father Callahan wouldn't let him dig the graves in the Precious Blood Cemetery if he didn't. He quit school at fourteen, the day he legally could in 1914, did farm work though a small hired hand and odd jobs thereafter, then enlisted at seventeen and went off to The Big War. And Biddy died. "Of natural causes," old Doc Dempsey the County Coroner ruled. "All bloated up," Eddie's heard, when found by an MPSP&P brakeman who used to stop and see her sometimes—"just visit with her" Ceil said when Eddie, curious, once asked about Banty's ma and her demise.

Frank Pratt while having a second piece of one of Bee's fresh-baked apple pies—a day or so after Sylvia Bremer had the baby boy she calls Bert—made a major philosophical pronouncement regarding all this. "Biddy Shanahan, before my time here but I know the story, now Syl Bremer," Frank said, irritating Ceil, "I guess you don't have to live in a big city, you want to encounter sin and some life's tragedies. We got plenty right here in little old Stiles."

T.R. St. George

Eddie, harking to Frank's pronouncement, felt better then for a time about living in Stiles, a place his Devlin cousins in Winatchee Falls, sneering, call a "one-horse burg."

Bee Heaney calls Banty, just turned thirty, he must have a real name but nobody seems to know what it is, a "poor old batch," meaning bachelor. He looks older on account of being shell-shocked in The Big War. He cooks his own meals, eats stuff out of cans he warms up mostly, and spends most of his free waking hours at the poolhall, a garrulous authority on just about anything, generous once a month when he gets his Veteran's Pension, quick then to buy everybody a near beer or bottle of pop before, predictable as the tides, he goes on a little spree with Steve (Packy) Wilson and a bottle of bootleg whiskey. Packy also gets a Veteran's Pension. His left arm was blown clean off at the shoulder in The Big War. He wears the shirtsleeves and coatsleeves he doesn't need folded up and pinned together. Packy's a permanent unwelcome handicapped hired man at his brother Lew's failing farm in the Winatchee River bottomlands but comes to Stiles once a month to get his Veteran's Pension check at the Post Office, cash it at the poolhall, go on a little spree with Banty and, predictable as the tides, slumped in one of the broken chairs in front of the poolhall late in the afternoon, pee in his pants. Stiles kids often witness this, wait for it in fact—a grown man peeing in his pants, a dark stain spreading slowly across Packy's crotch—with mixed shock and glee. Eddie guesses it's one of those horrors of war he's heard about.

"French champagne," Banty says, "you got to look at the bubbles. There's lots bubbles it's the good stuff. No bubbles, it taste like piss."

But French champagne, whatever its quality, holds no interest for Eddie. It's what men in those funny suits they call tuxedos and women in dresses that barely cover them drink in movies, and he's promised Ceil—she didn't name him Temperance for nothing, thrilling Old Tim Heaney, and there's that $250 in The Estate for advanced schooling to think about—he'll never drink beer or wine or liquor or champagne or anything. Hack Devlin promised that too: he Took The Pledge when he married Ceil but sometimes slips a little.

Old Tim's Estate

All the Devlins were and most of them still are drinkers. Uncle Dick Devlin for one. He was in The Big War too. He was pretty old for it but he was a U.S. Marine, gassed like Banty Shanahan but he wasn't shell-shocked or if he was he got over it, and he's got a pair of binoculars he took off a dead German officer in the Argonne Forest he sometimes lets Eddie looks through. Gassed or not, Uncle Dick still smokes two packs of Camels a day and goes on a little spree now and then. He was supposed to get married after the war but his sweetheart, Sheila Burns, one of the Burns girls, no patriot, married a German, Herman Strudel, the cheese-maker at the Simpson cheese factory, while Uncle Dick was in France. Uncle Dick, it's thought, won't ever get over that. He's the last Devlin born who survived and will likely be an old batch for the rest of his life. He sells cars for Joe (Cheesy) Adams, the crooked Dodge-Plymouth dealer in Winatchee Falls and, like Timothy J. Heaney, always comes to the Fourth of July Picnic at Precious Blood in a brand new car, the "demonstrator" he gets to drive.

Granny Devlin usually comes with him. She's Eddie's principal link to the past: all those distant years before he was born. She's really old, she'll soon be eighty-five, and wrinkled and her hair is white but she's still, it's said, "pretty spry and pretty sharp upstairs." Not a hundred percent but pretty close. She used to be a Connolly. She has eight kids, three died when they were little, a whole bunch of grandkids and a few great-grandkids. She has one daughter, Eddie's only heard about her, who's a nun, Sister Clementine, somewhere in Iowa. She's the next best thing to a son who's a priest. Granny Devlin was only six years old when she came to America from County Mayo with her folks, on a sailing ship, but still remembers that or claims to. The ship ran out of wind and was stuck in the ocean for a week, three-hundred miles from New York. It ran out of food too and the passengers on it were just about ready to draw lots to see which young single man they'd kill, chop up, cook and eat—but the crew caught some fish and the wind came back so they didn't have to eat anybody. Still, that's a pretty scary story or was anyway the first time Eddie heard it. He's heard it about fifty times by now. Granny Devlin tells it just about every time she sees him, though she sometimes thinks he's Mickey Devlin.

Uncle Dick usually slips Eddie a quarter at the Fourth of July picnic and one of Eddie's career plans, insofar as he has any, is to sell cars when he grows up and get to drive a demonstrator. That's if he doesn't go into aviation. Another career option of course is firemen. His Uncle Dan Devlin's a Winatchee Falls firemen and gets to slide down the pole in the Fire Hall and ride on the big red LaFrance fire engine when there's a fire or a false alarm even—a career a cowboy might envy.

But all these careers are some years off. Eddie leaves the poolhall, it's getting onto five p.m., and runs into one-eyed Petey Bremer, sniffling following a difference of opinion with his brother Kerm. Kerm hit him, Petey sniffles, and he wants to tell their dad that, "tell on" Kerm in the absence of any conflicting report from Kerm. Eddie gives Petey a ride on the handlebars on his bike down the dirt road beside the lumberyard to the MSP&P Section Gang shack beside the Main Line tracks. The Section Gang is Stiles' principal employer with five men, Werner Bremer's one of them, on its payroll. It patrols, maintains and repairs a twenty-mile stretch of MSP&P track and quits work at five p.m.

The Section Gang's pulling in on its puddle-jumper, a little flatcar with a two-stroke gasoline engine, when Eddie and Petey reach the shack. Milo Stacowitz, a big burly Polack, runs the Section Gang. He's the foreman and moved to Stiles from Winona in July with his wife and daughter, Lorrie, when promoted to foreman. Lorrie's a cute blonde girl, smart in school, who Eddie sometimes thinks he might like if ever he's inclined to like a girl, though that's doubtful. The other men on the Section Gang are Franz Geist (a stocky little German), Barney Poole (a big black Irishman) and his son Marlin, nineteen, big and muscular like Barney and the strongest person Eddie knows. Marlin can do twenty pull-ups with one-arm—without even puffing! Eddie can barely do four with both arms. Marlin's built up

Old Tim's Estate

his muscles working on the Section Gang, lifting oak ties, shoveling sand and ballast, heaving 800-pound rails with a crowbar, swinging a twenty-pound sledgehammer, pounding in the heavy spikes that clamp the rails to the ties.

The Section Gang pushes the puddle-jumper—piled with old ties, shovels, crowbars, pickaxes and sledgehammers—into the shack. Milo Stacowitz locks the padlock on the door and Petey tells on Kerm but gets little sympathy.

"I don't you snitching vant," Werner Bremer says, "You go home and out with your brother it work. Tell your ma I be the poolhall awhile." Werner Bremer's the only halfway skinny man on the Section Gang but also very strong—you have to be to do that kind of work. Barney Poole and Marlin also head for the poolhall: they always do. Milo Stacowitz and Franz Geist go home. They drink some kind of home brew they make in their cellars. Milo calls near beer "horse piss" and Franz Geist can't afford the poolhall, he has nine mouths to feed counting his own and his wife's. The Geists are the second biggest family in Stiles. The Murphy's are the biggest: there are ten of them but Bert's not around much since Sylvia Bremer had her baby. Their dad, Jiggs, drives a road-grader for the county in the summer and a snowplow in the winter. The Geists and the Murphys have big gardens and eat lots of cabbage and potatoes and turnips and squash and rutabagas they grow and the Geist kids and the Murphy kids think a slice of bread their ma bakes and slathers with lard is a big treat.

Petey's still sniffling. Eddie boosts him up on the handlebars and rides him back to the poolhall, then, nothing much else to do, rides home, where he finds Bee, armed with a dull hatchet, chasing a fat scared hen in the chicken yard beside the Devlins' garage. Just about everybody in Stiles keeps chickens, eats the eggs they lay and eats them. Bee and the Devlins have around thirty Rhode Island Reds, some are "spring chickens" hatched in April, the rest older, and an old rooster who along with all the other old roosters in Stiles greets each dawn. The chickens sleep in a coop in their yard, fenced with chicken wire and splattered with chicken poop, and Bee kills one just about every Saturday for Sunday dinner.

Eddie helps catch the scared squawking hen. Bee grabs its legs, lays it neck on a round oak block dark with blood, chops off its head with a single blow and turns it loose. The hen flops around for awhile without a head, its neck spurting blood, then collapses. This is a phenomenon Eddie's watched a hundred times but it still intrigues him. Can the hen's head see the rest of its former self flopping around? He once heard Banty Shanahan say the heads the French cut off people with a gillteen can do that. "They opical nerves and they brains," Banty said, "they ain't dead yet for about three seconds and they can see theresells, dead," though how Banty or anybody else figured that out is a mystery. And it's hard to tell about a chicken with a brain about as big as a pea. Bee picks up the hen—she'll cut off its legs, soak it in boiling water, pluck its feathers, remove its insides, another fairly interesting thing to watch, roast it Sunday morning—and they go into the house.

Ceil no doubt will ask Eddie, she always does, Where were you all afternoon? What did you do? Oh just around, Eddie will tell her, with Buddy mostly, nuthin' much. The old Forney place is forbidden. There might be hobos there who might hurt Eddie, Ceil says. She offers no details.

But Ceil for once doesn't ask Eddie anything. She's just off the phone, Estelle Heaney called, with a hot news flash. "They found Tim's car! In Fairbow! Young Charlie Goggins, Gert's boy, the policeman, found it. Go tell your Dad, Eddie! Estelle thinks somebody should go right over there. She thinks Tim might still be there!"

That's the message Ceil decoded. What Estelle, wary of rubberneckers, actually said was, "Aunt Gert just called me. That man with the Buick, the one Hack said he'd like to take a look at? It's in Fairbow. Gert's boy, Young Charlie, saw it. Do you think Hack could go right over there and take a look at it? The uh man might still be there!"

Old Tim's Estate

They make the forty-mile trip to Fairbow in Herb Bender's new car, a black '26 Chevy four-door Herb bought used a month ago from Cheesy Adams for $215 after Dick Devlin convinced him the tires were "like new," though there is no spare. Herb forgot to ask or look in the trunk. Except it's not a Ford, the Chevy's a pretty snappy car. It has a glass radiator cap with a red warning mark that shows the water temperature inside the radiator and a chrome spotlight beside the driver's window and all the windows roll up and down. Eddie, alone in the backseat, rolls the rear windows up and down until Hack tells him not to, he'll wear out the gears, and he dearly would like to fool with the spotlight but the driver, Herb, controls that.

Herb was drafted for this expedition, as was Hack, who though muttering some agreed under the circumstances to postpone his and Al's and Ernie's plan to mount the engine in the airplane-under-construction after supper. Bee phoned Herb and drafted him, disclosing a somewhat laundered version of the family secret. "We think our brother Tim had some car trouble over in Fairbow and Hack's going over there." Ceil didn't think Hack should go by himself and Bee agreed. Unspoken, at least in Eddie's presence, was the vague fear that Timothy J. Heaney, if found and under a lot of stress lately, might prove recalcitrant or something. Herb, he's a willing fellow, said Sure, soon's he finished milking and squared it with his mother, old Mrs. Bender, and got one of the Campion girls to come stay with her, she won't stay alone after dark. Old Mrs. Bender, she's coming up on ninety, no doubt gave Herb holy hell, that Hack's assessment, but Herb's got an independent streak in him that surfaces now and then and he really likes Bee. He's a sturdy little fellow with a farmer tan who wiped the manure from his shoes and put on his new bib overalls for this trip to Fairbow. He'd marry Bee in a minute if she could stand his mother and vice versa. Marry her anyway maybe except old Mrs. Bender holds the title to their farm and any time Herb mentions marriage or Bee she has a fit and threatens to throw Herb off the place and work it on shares with somebody else. Hack calls old Mrs. Bender "a certified case." Ceil and Bee call her "an old battle-ax."

T.R. St. George

Herb also offered to do the driving in his new Chevy and Hack agreed to that. Hack's a Ford man but considered the Chevy marginally more reliable than the Devlins' Model T. There's a tire on the T he doubted would "hold up" for another eighty miles. The Timothy J. Heaneys could not undertake this trip themselves. Estelle doesn't drive, neither does Edith at seventeen, and Bergda, while she drives, doesn't drive at night and was said to be in "no state" to drive anyway. There never was any suggestion Ceil or Bee accompany this expedition. It was a man's job—and a boy's, Eddie said. He whined and pleaded long and persistently, saying he'd help look for Uncle Tim, six eyes better than four and so on. Hack and Herb, Herb's pretty good to Eddie, said they'd keep an eye on Eddie and Ceil, she still has a miserable headache and was otherwise distraught, finally gave in and said Eddie could go along though it'll be way past his bedtime when he finally gets to bed.

Bee pried a snapshot of Tim at a Fourth of July Picnic out of the family album, it's ten years old but Tim's not changed much, Herb put gas in the Chevy, filled it up with Regular at Hack's pump, no charge, and away they went.

Chugging along on the gravel road to Fairbow, through Judgment (unincorporated like Stiles), Hayfield (incorporated), Racine and Dexter (likewise unincorporated) at a steady 35 mph—it says 80 on the Chevy's speedometer but Herb's a cautious driver, thinks 35 mph the ultimate nighttime speed and it's dark now—Eddie revives his kidnap theory. The kidnappers probably grabbed Uncle Tim when he was getting out of his Buick behind his office and made him drive to Fairbow, where they abandoned the Buick and now have Uncle Tim bound-and-gagged-tied-hand-and-foot somewhere. A hotel maybe. Finding him may present a problem but Ace Private Eye Bulldog Devlin's imagination skips that hurdle. When they do, he'll swiftly dispatch the kidnappers with a few lethal blows, no doubt surprising Herb and his dad with his prowess in the martial arts—

"What's Tim doing stuck in Fairbow?" Herb says, "He had car trouble, whyn't he just take his car some garrige?"

Old Tim's Estate

"Dammed if I know," Hack says, "All Tim's daughter Estelle told Ceil was Young Charlie Goggins, Gert Goggins' boy, Tim's nephew, he's a cop, he found Tim's Buick and knows where it is. Estelle's pretty cagey, talking on the phone, she thinks there's rubberneckers. We'll have to talk to Young Charlie, get the whole story."

"What whole story?" Herb says.

"Well," Hack says, "I don't know exactly what Bee told you, Herb, but Tim never showed up at his office yesterday. He left his house like usual but never went to his office. His office girl called Bergda. You know, Tim's wife. Office girl said there was somebody from an insurance company in the office wanted to see Tim and Bergda phoned some places but Tim wasn't any those places either. His car wasn't where he parks it. And he never came home for supper. Dinner, they call it. Fact is, the Heaneys don't know where Tim is and neither do we. Looks like he might be in Fairbow though. Might had some car trouble. Don't ask me why he dint just take it some garage. Or phone Bergda."

"He might been kidnapped," Eddie says.

"Oh forget that!" Hack says, "Your imagination's running wild, Eddie. Tell you the truth, Herb, we don't know what the hell's going on. Heaneys say Tim was in the Stock Market—"

"When it Crash?"

"Yeah, I guess. Prolly. I don't know for sure."

"Crash knock the starch out some, I guess," Herb says, "What I hear anyway. Where we wanna go then, we get inna town?" They're driving by the sprawling B&P Meat Packing Co. plant on Fairbow's outskirts, a vast brick structure that smells like dead meat, Fairbow's chief claim to fame. B&P stands for J.P. Burke and P.J. Peters, also known as Beef and Pork, competing butchers who in their late twenties, embracing efficiency, built in 1904 and began to share a slaughterhouse that grew and grew and grew until now the B&P Meat Packing Co. is said to be the tenth-largest meat-packing company in the country.—a true American success story.

"Gert Goggins' house," Hack says, "I don't know where Young

Charlie lives. Gert's house is over the south side. Take a left we get to Main Street and a right on Eighth Street."

Fairbow's a small city on flat ground on both banks of the Windy River, just a bit smaller (or larger) populationwise than Winatchee Falls: the 1930 Census will settle this burning question. Downtown, Main Street, looks a lot like Broadway in Winatchee Falls, a dozen blocks of two- and a few three-story buildings, but there's no world-famous Chiropractic Clinic. Fairbow's other claim to fame is that it was a "place" long before Winatchee Falls existed. It's named after Pierre Faribault, a French fur-trader who came up the Windy River in his canoe in the mid-1500s and for a time until the British drove him out ran a trading post (where it's said the Fairbow City Hall now stands), trading with the Sioux, trading whiskey for beaver pelts and nubile Sioux maidens.

Fairbow's working class live on the south side. Gert Goggins is home alone. Her husband, Old Charlie Goggins, is on the second-shift hog-kill and clean-up at the B&P and her daughter Celeste, twenty-four, who still lives at home and sells ladies' ready-to-wear someplace, has a Saturday night date. Eddie's been in this house before, the families visit back and forth some. It's just a house. Gert's a tall thin worried-looking woman like Ceil. She says with little enthusiasm she'll make coffee and doesn't offer Eddie anything. Hack and Herb decline the coffee, they want to talk to Young Charlie about Tim Heaney's Buick but don't know where Young Charlie lives. Gert goes on for quite awhile then about Tim, where is he, what got into him and so on and why didn't anybody tell her or Nell, their own brother, they wouldn't know yet probably except Young Charlie found Tim's car and phoned her and she was afraid Tim might had a heart attack or something and wondered what he was doing in Fairbow, so she called Estelle at work, S. Dolan & Sons, a long-distance call she supposes the Goggins will have to pay for. She seems to blame Hack for all this trouble. Hack says he guesses Ceil and Bee thought the Winatchee Falls Heaneys would tell her Tim was or is, well, missing—

"Oh, sure, those Heaneys!" Gert says, four bitter words that sum up her views on the way rich relatives treat their poor relations.

Old Tim's Estate

"That Estelle! I finally got it out of her, they don't know where Tim is!" Then she gives them directions to Young Charlie's house, three blocks away, though he may be bowling in the Police League.

Young Charlie's not bowling however. A husky young fellow in his late-twenties, 6-2 and 220 pounds in his socks, he favors the Goggins clan, he's at home, sitting at his kitchen table in his uniform pants and a dirty undershirt, trying to put his police issue .38 caliber revolver back together after cleaning it, a procedure that fascinates Eddie, while his wife Yegga, she's some kind of Bohunk, her antecedents suspect, battles with a squalling infant, either a boy or a girl, who does not want to go to bed.

Young Charlie Goggins trying to put his revolver back together.

T.R. St. George

"Police League bowls Tuesday nights," Young Charlie says, after Hack explains the purpose of their visit, "There's open bowling Sattiday nights. Tim's Buick now. Well, what happen. Yegga, shut the goddamn kid up! What happen, the Bus Depot call the station and report a car parked in its No Parking Zone and I was onna Parking Detail so I got over the Depot and it's a '29 Buick four-door and it look sort of familiar to me. Like I seen it before. Then I see them initials on the door, TJH, like Tim allas gets painted on his cars. I seen them the Precious Blood Fourth July picnic, Tim show me his new Buick, and I think, cripes, it might be Tim's Buick. So I look in the front seat, Buick wasn't lock, and there some letters there address Tim. So I figure it is Tim's Buick. I wunner what's he doin' in Fairbow and stall around awhile, think he might come get his Buick. But he dint. So finally I hadda call the tow-truck. Get it towed. Buick's down the Impound Lot. Somebody gonna have to pay the parking ticket and the tow charge, be four bucks altogether, get it out the Impound. Or I maybe can fix the ticket. Not'll Monday though. Impound's closed weekends. I ask a few questions too, the Bus Depot, anybody seen the fellow park the Buick, and kind of like describe Tim. One the ticket agents, Ricky Smiley, he said he might seen an older man, well-dressed, fit that description. But he wasn't sure. Then, I go off shift, I call ma and tell her I hadda impound Tim's Buick and I guess she call the Heaneys. What the hell's goin' on anyway?"

"We don't exactly know, Charlie," Hack says, "All we know is Tim left home yesterday like he always does, go his office. But he dint show up his office and nobody, nobody inna family I mean, seen or heard from him since."

"He might," Eddie says, "been kidnapped—"

"Oh for god's sake, Eddie, forget that!" Hack says. "Suppose we'll have to make another trip, get the damn Buick, we don't find Tim."

"They seen him the Bus Depot," Herb says, "Might seen him, I mean. He might took a bus and went somewheres. Went home—"

"That don't make any sense," Hack says, "he had his car, even it broke down. Or he took a bus, he be home by now. Anyway, we got a

Old Tim's Estate

picture Tim. Snapshot. I guess we might's well go down the Bus Depot, show it the agents there, this Smiley you mention. Some the hotels."

Young Charlie yawns and says that sounds to him like the next logical step in the investigation. "Smiley still be the Depot. He works the late shift, last bus leaves. Oh uh incidennly. Them letters was in Tim's Buick. I got them. I dint wanna leave them there so I took them. But I better give them you, Hack. I only glance them. They was open. It look like there some insurance companies after Tim. Claim he owe them for preemums or something."

Young Charlie lets Eddie hold his .38, put back together again finally though there seems to be a part left over and not loaded—Buddy Douglas will turn bright green with envy when he hears about that—goes into his bedroom and returns with the letters. There are four, dispatched by the Prudential, Metropolitan, Mutual of Omaha and Illinois Benevolent insurance companies. Hack stuffs them in his coat pocket. The infant's shut up and gone to sleep finally and Yegga, a stocky blonde woman with another infant in her stomach the way it looks, says she'll make coffee, but Hack and Herb decline this offer, thank Young Charlie, make Eddie relinquish the .38 and they head for the Bus Depot.

The Depot's a one-story tan brick building on the ragged south edge of downtown with Bus Parking Only signs in front of it. Inside there are a few hard benches, empty, a row of metal luggage lockers and a counter with a Purchase Tickets sign on it. Ricky Smiley's the agent on duty behind the counter—a weary sophisticate in his midtwenties with world-class pimples and a struggling mustache, wearing a grimy white shirt with a black rubber bowtie snapped to its wilted collar.

"What'd he do?" Ricky Smiley, studying Timothy J. Heaney's snapshot while squeezing a pimple, says, "Run off wit some farmer's daughter?"

"No," Hack Devlin says, "Mister Heaney's a respected Winatchee Falls businessman. He owns an insurance agency. We're kind of related him. We think he might had car trouble, took a bus. Police found his car outside the Depot here—"

"Oh yeah, Buick they tow," Ricky Smiley says, "Well, I think I seen him. Somebody look like him anyway. Yesserday or maybe t'day when I come work. I dint sell him no ticket though. Maybe Paulie, he's the agent-in-charge, might of. Lemme ast. Yo! Paulie!"

Paulie, a bald middle-aged man with a paunch and red suspenders, emerges from the office behind the counter and, apprised of the situation, studies Timothy J. Heaney's snapshot, doubts he "sold this gentleman a ticket," then snaps his fat fingers. "Say! I'm not sure but I believe I saw this gentleman about an hour ago. Over the Crystal Lunch. Diner right across the street there. I was over the Crystal my coffee break".

This, Eddie knows, is a "hot clue." He sometimes reads Ernie Hoff's True Detective Magazines, looks at the pictures anyway, which Ernie considers some of the World's Great Literature. Hack and Herb also consider this a hot clue. Eddie grabs some bus schedules from a rack on the counter and they cross the street to the Crystal Lunch, a diner with a red neon sign on its roof, Open 24 Hours, and inside a long counter and a few booths. Hack queries the counterman, also the executive chef, a skinny man in a greasy apron with a cigarette hung on his lower lip.

"Well I ain't positive sure," the chef, studying Timothy J. Heaney's snapshot, says. "But I think this guy was in here supper. Somebody look like him anyway. Dinner too. I weren't here breakfast. I think I hear him say he stayin' the Star Hotel. Other side the Bus Depot there."

Another hot clue! They're closing fast on their quarry and his kidnappers in Ace Private Eye Bulldog Devlin's expert opinion, and Buddy Douglas' belly-button will turn inside out with envy when he hears all about this adventure.

The Star Hotel is a seedy establishment in an old two-story brick building a block beyond the Bus Depot. It's tiny lobby smells of old socks and cheap cigar smoke. The night clerk on duty, half-asleep on

Old Tim's Estate

his feet behind the minimal front desk, may be Ricky Smiley's brother, they bear a striking pimply resemblance at any rate, though this one's wearing a brown plaid shirt and stringy frog-green tie—and Timothy J. Heaney of Winatchee Falls is a registered guest, checked in at three p.m. Friday.

"Must had some luggage wit him," the night clerk, studying Tim's registration, says. "Dint pay in advance and that's a rule we got. I guess he's up his room. Key ain't here. You can go on up, you wanna, knock onna door. Nummer twenty-two."

Hack and Herb and Eddie go up a rickety stairway behind the front desk and find Number 22 at the end of a dimly lit hall. Hack knocks on the door. There's no response. Hack knocks again with no result. Ace Private Eye Bulldog Devlin flexes his hands, lethal weapons, prepared for action should a kidnapper open the door. No doubt the kidnappers made Uncle Tim get a room in the Star Hotel, that procedure's not part of Bulldog's expertise, and are in the room with him. Hack bangs on the door with no result, then tries the doorknob. Number 22 is locked and they return down the rickety stairs to the lobby.

"Well he seem okay t'me," the night clerk, told Timothy J. Heaney may be sick or something, says. "I owny seen him a minute, guess it was him, he come down this morning. I goes off at eight o'clock." And he won't unlock Number 22 with his master key. "Management kill me, I do that. That's another rule we got. Some our guess, y'know, they got guess sometimes. Y'know, wimmin? Star Hotel protect their privacy. Or else Mister Heaney prolly just out some place. Should left his key but guess fergit. You can wait for him, you wanna. Can't sleep inna lobby though. That's another rule."

Hack and Herb confer and decide they'll wait, wait awhile anyway. Eddie says he's hungry, he saw a chocolate cake in a glass case at the Crystal Lunch he'd like to sample, but Hack says they'll wait awhile for Tim then get something to eat. He phones Ceil, collect, using the phone at the front desk ("No long-distance calls 'cept collect," the night clerk says, another rule) and tells Ceil, "It looks like we found

89

T.R. St. George

Tim one the hotels. But he ain't in his room so we'll wait awhile, he comes back." Oh Thank God! Ceil says, She'll phone Estelle right away with this good news and is there anywhere Eddie can sleep? Hack says Eddie's fine.

They wait in the Star Hotel lobby on a greasy moth-eaten couch and an equally greasy moth-eaten overstuffed chair, those and two spittoons and a rubber plant that's seen better days the only furnishings. Herb leafs through what's left of an abandoned Fairbow Daily Herald, checking the calf, yearling steer, heifer, prime hog, gilt and pork belly prices the B&P was paying Thursday. Hack pulls up a spittoon, fits a pinch of Red Dog in his cheek (Hack likes a chew now and then though Ceil thinks that a "disgusting habit") and takes a look at the letters Young Charlie found in Tim's Buick, Timothy J. Heaney's mail but what the hell, under the circumstances—

"Jumping Jeezuzz!" Hack says, which is not exactly the Lord's name, "There some insurance companies after Tim all right! Claim he owes them, lemma see, four and six and nine and. . . . Jeezuzz! Owes them twenty-six hundred dollars for premiums!"

Herb has no comment, that's not any of his business. Hack puts the letters back in his pocket and Bulldog Devlin, sharing the greasy couch with Hack, soon grows restless. Stakeouts (and this is a stakeout, Bulldog figures, or close enough, though Uncle Tim's not a Wanted Criminal or Prime Suspect) are always boring but part of the job. True Detective authors often note this fact. He wishes he had a True Detective, something with pictures in it to pass the time, and wonders why anybody, anybody in their right mind anyway, would share their hotel room with a woman—if they didn't have to? He again tells Hack he's hungry, but Hack says, No, they'll wait awhile yet, Tim might come in any minute.

They wait another hour. It's past eleven o'clock. Stakeouts are a pain in the neck and it's been a long day and, up until now, an exciting one. It's not very exciting now though and Bulldog Devlin's eyes, he can't help it, slowly close—

"Hey! Kid can't sleep in the lobby!" the night clerk says, "That's

Old Tim's Estate

a rule. Management kill me, kid sleeps inna lobby. Kid gonna sleep, you gotta get a room."

Hack relents then, the night clerk says he'll "keep an eye out" for Mr. Heaney, tell him he has company, and they walk to the Crystal Lunch, which is pretty much deserted. "Find that fella yer was lookin' for?" the chef asks. No, Hack says, but he's registered the Star Hotel, just out for the evening, I guess. The counterman grunts, Hack and Herb have pie and coffee and Eddie has a glass of milk and a piece of the chocolate cake. It's pretty exciting, eating in a restaurant in the middle of the night and Buddy Douglas will hear all about it, but the chocolate cake's a big disappointment. It looks better than it tastes and it's not really very chocolly. They might of put some artificial color in it. Bee's cakes are far better. Nevertheless, Eddie's eats this cake, he's been told a thousand times he mustn't "waste food," then pees at the Crystal Lunch—another indoor bathroom but a far cry from the others he's peed in. He has to pee in one of those things on the wall called a "yournal," which he barely can reach. It's full of other people's pee and things like mothballs, they may be mothballs, and the whole place smells worse even than the B&P Meat Packing plant. Different, but worse.

Hack and Herb pee too, then they go get the Chevy, Herb parked it in a Parking Zone near the Bus Depot, and park it outside the Star Hotel. Herb says he can wait awhile yet for Tim Heaney but has to get home by six o'clock, milk his cows, and maybe Eddie, he looks pretty pooped, can sleep in the Chevy. Eddie's just about ready to climb into the Chevy's rear seat and curl up under a smelly horse-blanket Herb pulls from the trunk when Hack says, "Lemme try that night clerk again, see he'll unlock Tim's door."

They go into the Star Hotel lobby. Hack takes a $1 bill from his wallet, he's got $3 left, lays the $1 on the front desk and explains: Mr. Timothy J. Heaney's a highly respected Winatchee Falls businessman who owns an insurance agency, he was in the Stock Market and there's not one chance in a thousand Mr. Heaney has a wo—guest in his room. "I know him," Hack says, "I'm one his brothers-in- law." But Mr.

Heaney's "not real well." He's been "under a lot of stress lately" and he might had a heart attack or something. "Be a terrible thing, Mister Heaney had a heart attack or something here the Star Hotel and nobody even take the trouble, find out he's dead or alive."

The night clerk, swift as a striking rattlesnake, pockets the dollar. "Oh, well, that case," he says, "a medical emergency like. That's a diff'rent story. You promise you never tell the management, we'll go up, take a look his room."

Hack promises, though he doesn't cross his heart and hope to die, and the night clerk gets his master key and they go up the rickety stairs and the night clerk opens Number 22. It's empty, the lights on, the bedclothes all tangled, candy wrappers here and there, an ashtray full of cigar butts on the window sill, a cheap straw suitcase on the floor at the foot of the bed. Bulldog Devlin inventories these clues but they don't tell him much. There's nobody in the bathroom either since there is no bathroom, that's a communal facility down the hall, but there's a note scrawled on a Webber Investments envelope propped against the cloudy mirror on a battered chest of drawers. The night clerk reads it.

"Oh shit!" he says, swearing in Eddie's presence, "The sonofabitch skipped! Stiffed us a day's rate! Two, he skipped after check-out, 'leven o'clock!"

"I don't think he skipped," Herb says, "suitcase still here."

The night clerk grabs the suitcase. It flops open, empty. "Be dammed!" he says, "the old empty suitcase trick! And the day guy fell for it! Be his ass! No, guy was here skipped awright. Lookit this fuckin' note!" Hack and Herb read the note, then let Eddie read Timothy J. Heaney's spidery scrawl:

> Star Hotel Management:
> I regret to advise that I am somewhat short of cash at this time and will need the cash I have for a lengthy bus trip. You may, however, expect my

Old Tim's Estate

>check for One Day's Occupancy in full in the very near future.
>
>>Timothy J. Heaney, Esq.

The night clerk's still chuckling, enjoying the day man's upcoming discomfiture and probable punishment when they leave the Star Hotel and Hack and Herb, confronted by what appears to be a dead end in the investigation—often the case though only temporarily in True Detective sagas—confer beside the Chevy.

"Left his car, skipped out the hotel," Herb says, "Look to me like Tim's gone. Up and flew the coop somewhere. Prolly took a bus. One the agents the Bus Depot prolly sold him a ticket. They might remember where, we ask them again."

But Paulie, the agent-in-charge, has gone home, nobody left at the Depot but Ricky Smiley and he's closing up: the last Greyhound left for Mason City, Des Moines, Council Bluffs, Omaha and points west ten minutes ago. Nor can he, Ricky says, reveal Paulie's address, "where he lives," or phone number. "That's a company rule. Anyway, we sells sixty, sevenny tickets a day, some days, and Paulie, his memory sort of goin', y'know what I mean."

So much for that then. They leave the Bus Depot and Hack and Herb confer again beneath a streetlight. "Eddie," Hack says, "lemme see them bus schedules you grab." Eddie hands them over and Hack studies them. "Hell! There was buses left here for just about everwhere t'day! North south east west. Tim might took any them, he took a bus. To hell with it, Herb. Let's go home." Hack's swearing in Eddie's presence but he's tired, they're all tired. It's past midnight, Fairbow's streets are deserted, most of the downtown neon signs gone dark though the one that says CRY TAL LU CH Open 24 Hours still flickers.

"Suits me," Herb says, "but I better get another cup coffee the diner there first. Keep me awake I'm driving."

They get the Chevy, park it outside the Crystal Lunch, open twenty-four hours a day, and go into the Crystal, where a lone customer, a middle-aged man in a baggy suit on a stool at the end of the counter is staring at his coffee. The chef—still on duty, filling in for goddamn night man didn't show up, he says—leans across the counter. "Fella there the end the counter," he says, a hoarse whisper, "he the one I tell yer I seen dinner, supper. He the one yer lookin' for?"

Well, eyewitnesses are notoriously unreliable. Bulldog Devlin and True Detective authors know that to be a fact. The man at the counter resembles Timothy J. Heaney some as to age and build but has thick dark hair, while Timothy J. Heaney's as good as bald but for a thin gray fringe over his ears.

"No," Hack says, "ain't him. Just a coincidence, I guess, he stayin' the Star Hotel. Fellow we're lookin' for was at the Star too. But he uh well he check out."

Hack and Herb have coffee, nickel a cup with a free refill, Eddie's too tired to eat, and they leave and get into the Chevy and depart and Eddie's sound asleep under the smelly horse-blanket before they drive by the smelly B&P plant.

He wakes some unknown time later when the Chevy bumps off County Road O onto O's narrow shoulder somewhere in the middle of nowhere somewhere west of Hayfield with a flat tire, the left rear, one of the joys of motoring.

"We'll put the spare on," Hack says.

"There ain't no spare," Herb says.

"Oh shi—shucks!" Hack says, and Herb says some unkind things about Dick Devlin, then turns the Chevy's lights off so's not to run the battery down, and they climb out of the Chevy and roust Eddie out and he stands yawning and shivering, the night's turned chilly, in the darkness, no light in sight anywhere, everybody in Hayfield probably in bed, while Hack and Herb fix the flat. There's a half moon high in the southern sky, just enough light to work with. They dig Herb's jack, repair kit in a little cylindrical tin can, tire pump and a short oak plank out of the trunk, put the jack on the plank just forward of the flat, jack-up the Chevy, remove the lugnuts on the left rear wheel with the jack-handle and many muttered oaths, remove the wheel, pry the

Old Tim's Estate

tire off the rim, extract the red rubber innertube and search the tube for the puncture with Herb's dim dying flashlight. They find a hole no bigger than a pinhead. Hack, he's the expert, screws the top that looks like a tiny cheese-grater off the repair kit, scratches the innertube where the hole is, smears the stickum in the repair kit on the scratches, peels the white backing off one of the red rubber patches in the kit, presses the patch on the stickum and holds the patch tight with one thumb while the stickum dries and an MSP&P freight chugging out of Hayfield, chugging up a long grade on the Main Line, its headlight slicing the night, treats the dark countryside to a long lonely wailing whistle. The patch dries and Herb pumps some air into the innertube. This is the tricky part. There may be another puncture in the tube or the patch may leak. Neither's the case, thankfully. The freight chugs away to the west, trailing another long lonely wailing whistle, the red light on its caboose slowly fading from sight. Hack stuffs the innertube back in the tire, wrestles the tire onto the wheel rim, mounts the wheel on the brake drum, finds and replaces the lugnuts and screws them tight. Herb pumps the tube full of air. They lower the jack, put everything back in the trunk, climb into the Chevy and are on their way again on County O, Eddie sound asleep under the smelly horse-blanket in just about thirty seconds.

It's way past two a.m., the latest Eddie's ever been up, when Herb drops them off in Stiles, and he's sound asleep curled up in his cot in his shorts, too tired to dispatch any kidnappers and that theory's unraveling anyway when Hack Devlin begins his report on the failed expedition to Fairbow and Timothy J. Heaney's problem with those insurance companies.

3.

Sunday. Bee rousts Eddie out of a sound sleep at nine a.m. in time for the ten o'clock Mass at Precious Blood. Young Bernie Griffin's Catechism class only meets in the summer. Still half asleep, Eddie gets into his church clothes—his Whoopee pants, a clean sportshirt and his new sneakers—stumbles downstairs and gulps a glass of milk and a cookie. The old hen Bee killed is roasting in the oven, he can smell it, and Ceil will baste it. Ceil still has a miserable headache, didn't sleep a wink, really worried now about Tim and his premium problem, and doesn't "feel up" to mass. She'll stay home and say a Rosary and who knows, Estelle might call, there's any news.

Estelle learned of Tim's apparent brief sojourn in Fairbow (but nothing about his premium problem) at two-thirty a.m. Ceil phoned her collect, the second time within four hours, not bothering to encode her report, all the rubberneckers assumed to be in bed. Bergda was asleep, she took a pill so she could get some sleep, Estelle said, after Ceil in her first phone call, confusing any rubberneckers, said, "Hack had a look at that car and he's waiting for the man owns it to come back to his hotel." Estelle at two-thirty said she'd have to tell Bergda when she wakes up that man left his hotel for parts unknown and didn't know what poor Bergda would do then. Estelle sounded like she blamed Ceil for these conflicting reports: she was sort of snippety. She also said she'd phoned "the girls" finally—Edna in Albuquerque, Edwina in Boise—in clear, neither is on a party line,

Old Tim's Estate

and told them their father was, is, well, missing. Both naturally are said to be "terribly upset."

All this Eddie learns on the way to mass in the Model T, Hack and Bee discussing and updating the family mystery en route. He tries to picture Edna and Edwina as he vaguely remembers them "terribly upset." Are they standing on their heads then? Showing all their underwear?

Hack thinks Tim might be on his way to Omaha (or Chicago) to talk to those insurance companies, Mutual of Omaha (or Illinois Benevolent) that claim he owes them premiums. Hack also wonders what they should do with the letters, Tim's letters, Young Charlie Goggins gave him? Hack only glanced at them, see there might be a clue in them: Hack also reads True Detective. And Tim's premium problem may be a clue, though why Tim, thirty years in the insurance business, did not send those companies their premiums is a big mystery. But the letters were, are, Tim's personal mail. It might ruffle Estelle's feathers, they're easily ruffled, Bergda's too, if they knew Hack (and Ceil and Bee and Young Charlie Goggins) read Tim's personal mail. Hack's inclination is to do nothing with the letters, just put them somewhere and say nothing. But Young Charlie Goggins is privy to Tim's premium problem and Young Charlie's got a big mouth: he might spill the beans. Bee wonders is there some way they can paste the letters shut again, pretend nobody read them and send them to Estelle—mail them, save a trip to Winatchee Falls. But Hack doubts that's feasible, all the envelopes are torn. The upshot of all this is they decide to do nothing for the time being. Ceil will put the dammed letters in a safe place and leave it to Tim to work things out with the insurance companies.

"And we'll all say some prayers for Tim, we're at Mass," Bee says, "Pray he's all right, where ever he is."

Eddie says a little prayer ("Please, God, keep Uncle Tim safe") early in the Mass, then dozes off during Father Callahan's interminable sermon, something to do with the wonders the Holy Mother will bestow on all the faithful who have great faith in her and lots and lots of patience.

Mass over finally, Hack and other male faithful discuss corn prices and the dismal state of The Government and Bee and other female faithful exchange recipes and gossip. One bit of gossip is old Mac McCready, busy goddamning the goddamn Government though in the shadow of a House of the Lord, will soon at long last soon be grandfather. His daughter Mame, the one who screeched at Old Tim Heaney's funeral, married now, her husband's got a good steady job with the Cornbelt Foods Corporation somewhere in Iowa, is pregnant. Everybody's happy for old Mac, grouch though he be. They gave up on his other daughter Elsa years ago. She's way past thirty, has no beau, still lives at home, takes care of her mother who has the diabetes, missed Mass to stay with the old lady.

Eddie meanwhile gets into a tussling match with his some-kind-of-cousin Whip Rahilly and winds up with grass-stains all over his Whoopee pants. Whip came late to Mass with Slicky Riordan on Slicky's Harley. They arrived in time for the Gospel though, Eddie saw them ease into the church, so technically speaking they did not miss Mass, but they didn't sit in a pew. They stood in the back by the Confessional—a shoddy way to attend Mass, Ceil says, shows no respect for the Lord, but Father Callahan's nearsighted, can't see the Confessional from his pulpit—and ducked out early to smoke cigarettes.

On the way home, the Model T chugging along, Bee tells Eddie, "Soon's we get home, take your pants off. I'll put them in the wash so your mother won't see them." Ceil abhors grass-stains.

But Ceil's oblivious to grass-stains when they get home. Estelle phoned, not so snippety this time, not bothering to encode much, the rubberneckers thought to be at services. A "business acquaintance" of Tim's she ran into at the eleven o'clock Mass at Holy Redeemer thought he saw Tim in St. Paul on Saturday and wondered what Tim was doing there? Estelle, lying, said Tim had "some business" there and now she'd like to mount another search-and-rescue

Old Tim's Estate

operation—but fears St. Paul is too far away and too big to search successfully. Hack Devlin concurs with that assessment. Besides, he says, they know Tim was in Fairbow on Saturday, part of Saturday anyway, and old Mrs. Bender will never let Herb out two days running, maybe Estelle should just phone the police in St. Paul.

"Oh, Estelle will never do that," Ceil says, "and she was pretty snippety, two-thirty this morning." Nevertheless, she phones Estelle, collect, the Heaneys' phone bill is climbing, Bergda's still sleeping, and tells Estelle (blood may be thicker than water but family loyalty has to end somewhere) without much encoding, "I'm afraid a trip to St. Paul is out of the question. Hack was up half the night last night, you know. He thinks you should call the authorities in St. Paul."

But Estelle, Ceil reports when off the phone, said, No, absolutely not, the Heaneys don't want any authorities involved or any publicity for god's sake! It's bad enough without anybody else knowing anything about, well, the matter they've been discussing.

"What'd I tell you?" Ceil says, and that's the end of any expedition to St. Paul—there won't be one—and the Devlins, Bee, Frank and Ernie sit down to Sunday dinner: roast chicken with stuffing, mashed potatoes and gravy, some peas Bee canned and a rhubarb pie she (despite the family crisis) baked Saturday.

Dinner finished, Ceil goes upstairs to lie down: her miserable headache and the ongoing Timothy J. Heaney mystery are killing her. Bee gets busy washing the dishes. Frank goes back to the poolhall, Banty Shanahan in charge there, for a little nap prior to his Sunday night date with his mysterious lady friend in Winatchee Falls. Hack and Ernie slip away to meet Al Morris and finally mount the engine on the airplane-under-construction and Eddie, naturally, jumps on his bike and tags along: wild horses couldn't stop him.

Hack and Ernie, grunting, lift the hopped-up Model T engine onto a dolly in Hack's garage and roll it up the sidewalk to Al's Repair Shop, where Al hooks it to the block-and-tackle in the shop ceiling and hoists it up in front of the airplane's fuselage. Word that this

T.R. St. George

operation is underway spreads swiftly in the mysterious way news spreads swiftly in Stiles and there's soon a fair-sized curious crowd on hand watching. It's a big event and there's seldom much to do Sunday afternoon, or any afternoon, in Stiles. Lee J. Lilly shows up. So does Banty Shanahan, though he's supposed to be running the poolhall. Lenny Gibbons and Harry Kelly arrive still in their Sunday suits, followed by Poop Clarke, Buddy Douglas, his brother Ronnie, their father Bruce and sundry other adults. There also are numerous kids: Margie Bremer and her brothers, Kermit and one-eyed Petey, their sister Sylvia lugging the infant she calls Bert (both impervious to the curiosity their presence triggers), Hinty Murphy and his little brother Frankie, though they're supposed to be hunting the last squash in the Murphy's big garden. Old Tom Ticke passes by pushing a wheelbarrow full of trash but does not stop: the airplane doesn't interest Old Tom. Slicky Riordan and Whip Rahilly roar up on Slicky's Harley, trailing a cloud of dust, how they got the word more mysterious still, but it turns out they didn't, they were just out riding around and saw the crowd outside Al's shop.

Al won't let anybody in the shop. He and Hack and Ernie need "room to work," he says. So everybody watches from the door, the kids crowding up to the front so they can see. Throughout the summer and fall, Ernie's airplane has been a constant topic of interest in Stiles and now that it's nearing completion this interest is peaking. Many doubt the airplane will fly or that Ernie, though he claims to have had four flying lessons at the Winatchee Falls Airport, can fly it. But others, true believers in the future of aviation, cite the Wright Brothers and the airplane they built in their bicycle shop. Some bets have been placed. Banty Shanahan's bet $2, the going price for the digging of an adult grave, the airplane will fly, against Lee J. Lilly's $2 it won't. Poop Clarke's bet $1 it will against Harry Kelly's $1 it won't. No odds have been posted, but opinion is pretty evenly divided. And even those who doubt the airplane will fly, or that Ernie can fly it, may secretly hope it will and he can. An airplane built in Stiles, after all—if it flies, with a Stiles resident at the controls—will really be something!

Old Tim's Estate

Something no nearby unincorporated village—Simpson, Tilden, Predmore, Judgment, all bitter tribal rivals—can match or even hope to match, ever. Bragging rights for years to come are at stake.

In fact, Ernie's airplane, becoming a kind of common cause, along with the passage of time, has pretty much healed the rift that split Stiles like a 6.0-on-the-Richter-Scale-earthquake a year ago, when Alfred E. (Al) Smith, a Democrat and a Catholic, the first Catholic to seek the presidency of the United States, and Herbert Hoover, the incumbent, a Quaker, some kind of Protestant, were campaigning for the White House. (Prohibition when under discussion, Eddie's heard, also split the village, but he wasn't around for that.) Smith and Hoover sometimes talked on the radio though hard to hear through all the static, the Winatchee Falls Bugle Call was full of election news and politics and religion proved a lethal combination. The Protestant line in Stiles (and elsewhere), also espoused by agnostics, was Smith wins the damn Pope will be running the country! Kermit Bremer spouted that theory while twice beating up on Eddie when their political discussions led to blows. Feelings also ran high at the poolhall, where Marlin Poole, who still thinks he's a Catholic though he's not been to Mass for years except (some years) Christmas and Easter, twice threatened to shove Ernie Hoff's goddamn Hoover Button up Ernie's goddamn ass.

Frank Pratt finally had to lay down the law, forbidding political discussions. "Politics is bad enough," Frank, making another major philosophical pronouncement, said. "You mix politics and religion all you're gonna get is trouble."

Nor did the election itself (Hoover the big winner with 58.2 percent of the vote nationally) clear the air or heal this rift. Stiles, it's thought, "went for Smith," every blessed Catholic with the possible exception of Harry Kelly, a knee-jerk Republican, voting for Smith at the Tilden Township Town Hall a mile to the east on County Road O, while numerous Protestants and agnostics, though stout Hoover supporters, did not bother to vote. But nobody knows for sure. Stiles is unincorporated so its votes are lumped in with the rest of the Tilden Township vote. Tilden Township "went for Smith" by a narrow margin, a pyrrhic victory some Stiles Catholics cited for awhile. Hoover supporters considered that a dumb stubborn refusal to face the facts and the rift brought on by the election persisted. Time was healing this rift though at a glacial pace when in May the airplane came. Ernie soon thereafter began to build his airplane and aviation reunited Stiles—reunited it anyway as much as it's ever been united.

Al hoists the engine higher. Hack Devlin jiggles it into place inside the ash struts and onto the metal mounts already in place in the airplane's nose. Ernie hovers over him, offering bad advice. The fit is perfect, Hack and Al are true crafstman, the Wright Brothers incarnate. Hack bolts the engine to the mounts, wires it to the six-volt battery and connects the fuel line to the former Nash gas tank forward of the passenger seat, both installed earlier. Al fetches the propeller, slips it on the drive shaft and bolts it tight and Ernie, beaming, excited, gives the propeller a couple of twists. It twists satisfactorily. Banty Shanahan and a few kids applaud this technological marvel and Banty bets another $1 against Bruce Douglas' $1 (Bruce the Scot cautious with a dollar, that's his reputation anyway, but a skeptic like his son Buddy) the airplane will by god fly with Ernie at the controls! Nobody else applauds but the airplane as yet has no wings.

Ernie, hopping around with excitement, he's no phlegmatic German today, wants to start the engine and "sure make the propeller spin it vill," but Al scotches that idea. The airplane, he points out, has no brakes and will charge across the shop and wreck itself if under power. Hack assures Ernie the engine will start and spin the propeller: he'll stake his reputation on it. Ernie then suggests "vee out the shop from it poosh and der vings on put." But if they do that, Al points out, they can't put the airplane back in the shop, it won't fit, they'll have to roll it across the street to the lumberyard, where Ernie, restacking a lot of lumber, has made space he calls "der airplane hanger." Besides, Al's not put the instruments in the airplane yet.

Old Tim's Estate

"I'll put the instruments in tomorrow, Ernie," Al says, "then we'll roll it out, put the wings on, block the wheels and test the controls and the engine."

"Den I it fly vill!" Ernie says, "Oop it take! I your paster can use, Lenny? Vare it down sloop from der tracks across dere? Is easier der airplane to off-take I tink is vare it down sloop. Like dot fella der airplane came done?"

"Sure, welcome to it," Lenny Gibbons says, "Look out for my bull though. Then I guess you'll give me a ride in your airplane, huh? Or maybe I'll ride on the wings like that fella I saw the County Fair done." Lenny's a part-time humorist in high spirits who farms one-hundred-sixty acres beyond the MSP&P tracks, milks twenty Holstein and sells his milk and cream, collected by Poop Clarke, to the Co-op Dairy—in highs spirits because he got a letter yesterday from the MSP&P advising him that a Mr. Webster R. Allen, an MSP&P lawyer, will be in Stiles on Tuesday to settle for the blue-ribbon Holstein the freight killed nearly six months ago.

With that, nothing else to watch, the crowd breaks up. Al locks his shop and goes home. He's some kind of a Baptist, lives with his folks, they don't drink and Al usually won't work Sundays, but made an exception. Winter's coming, it could snow any day and he doesn't want the airplane cluttering up his shop until spring. Al also, though loathe to show it, is pretty excited about the airplane's first flight—his handiwork soaring through the clouds.

Most of the other adults retire to the poolhall, where Frank Pratt's shaving beside his potbellied stove in preparation for his Sunday night date. Banty Shanahan, money in his pocket, he dug two graves Saturday in the St. Olaf Cemetery in Predmore for adolescent twins carried off by the meningitis, buys several people a near beer or a bottle of pop, their choice, and expounds at some length on the tricky maneuvers required in aerial combat. Banty claims to have seen a lot of dogfights while he was in France. Sometimes in his war stories

T.R. St. George

Banty was a brave doughboy in the trenches, other times he was the machine-gunner in an airplane dropping bombs on the hated Huns, blowing them to bits. The local consensus is he was a brave doughboy but sometimes on account of being shell-shocked truly believes he was an airplane machine-gunner.

The Murphy kids go home to hunt squash and most of the other kids, pushy Margie Bremer among them, crowd around Slicky Riordan's Harley, admiring the 100 mph on its speedometer, asking Slicky how fast he's gone on it ("Even hundred," Slicky says) and hoping, slim though this hope be, he'll give them a ride on the Harley. And darned if Slicky doesn't give Margie Bremer a ride on it, up and down main street twice at 50 miles an hour, Margie's dirty blonde hair flying, her dress up around her bottom, her arms wrapped tight around Slicky. Slicky won't give anybody else a ride though, despite many pleas, and soon roars out of town on County O with Whip Rahilly on the buddyseat, trailing a cloud of dust.

Most of the kids go over to the park then, where Margie Bremer, now hated by all, climbs the biggest tree, all the way to the top, giving everybody a good look at her underpants, and Eddie and the other small boys race around with their arms outspread, executing tricky aerial maneuvers, making a noise, rup-rup-rup-rup, like the staccato chatter of a sinkernized machine-gun firing through a propeller, shooting each other down in flames, everybody soon an Ace three times over. They're all counting the hours until tomorrow afternoon, just about twenty-four, when Al Morris will put the wings on the airplane and Ernie will oop it take. Which, Kermit Bremer says, better not happen before school lets out or he for one will just skip school.

"Me too," Eddie says, thought Ceil will kill him, he skips school. But it may not come to that. School lets out at three-thirty, the farm kids have to go home and do chores, and Ernie's supposed to run the lumberyard until five p.m. It'll be almost dark by then, though. Ernie most likely will close the lumberyard early (his Frohoeft Co. boss in Winatchee Falls will never know) so he can goggle-up and fly his airplane in daylight. He'll ride his bike to school tomorrow, Eddie decides, and the minute school lets out race to Lenny Gibbons' pasture for an event, as he sees it, more or less the equivalent of the Wright Brothers' historic first flight at Kitty Hawk there was a picture of in The Weekly Reader. But he'll see this first flight and afterwards all the kids in Simpson, Judgment, Predmore and Tilden will be sick with envy. Forever. Simpson beat Stiles 21-2 in a softball game at their annual joint school picnic in Tilden State Park in May, Eddie going zip-for-four, four strikeouts, never got his bat off his shoulder, the Simpson pitcher a kid named Wolfe (Woofie) Strudel who looked to be about eighteen—and it's time to get even. Eddie's sure Ernie's airplane will fly. His dad after all built the engine: well, rebuilt it.

Woofie Strudel. He's another kid Eddie would like to kill, slowly, or beat up anyway, though Eddie mostly only considers this hopeless idea every other Sunday when (unless there's blizzard or frost boils) Woofie comes to the ten o'clock Mass at Precious Blood with his mother, the Burns girl who was supposed to marry Dick Devlin after The War but married Herman Strudel instead, while Dick was in France. She's supposed to raise Woofie a Catholic but there's no Catholic church in Simpson, just a Lutheran. Other Sundays Woofie and his dad go there. Woofie's only half a Catholic. That being the case, Eddie surmises, Woofie will wind up in Hell eventually. But that may be a long time coming: revenge for the softball shellacking long delayed. Eddie would like to kill Woofie or beat him up now. But Woofie like Hinty Murphy is twelve (he only looks like he's eighteen) and bigger and stronger than Eddie. He's not very tall but he's built up his muscles wrestling with milkcans full of milk at the Simpson cheese factory where his dad's the cheese-maker.

Were Woofie a hated Hun, Eddie thinks while ripping Petey Bremer's hated Fokker with a deadly burst of machine-gun fire (and Woofie after all is half a hated Hun) he'd shoot Woofie down in flames—then with another deadly burst blows the tail off Petey's hated Fokker.

But this aerial combat soon palls. Petey Bremer refuses to be shot down again though his hated Fokker clearly is in flames, then refuses to even be a hated Fokker anymore. A few kids throw sticks at Margie Bremer up in her tree, but can't throw far enough to hit her and desist when Margie yells they better stop or she'll come down and beat the crap out of them. Boredom sets in, but Hinty Murphy puts an end to that, riding up on his old bike with a hot news flash: "The Pooles're fightin'!"

Eddie jumps on his bike, puts Petey on the handlebars and along with the other kids, on foot and on bikes, follows Hinty back to his house, where they hide in the dried cornstalks in the Murphy's big garden. The Pooles live nextdoor in a beat-up old house with a sagging porch and watching the Pooles fight is something there is to do some Sunday afternoons in Stiles.

There are four Pooles: Barney and his son Marlin from the Section Gang, Marlin's sister Gail, she's twenty-one, and old Mrs. Poole, Barney's mother. Barney sometimes goes on a spree weekends with a bottle of bootleg whiskey. He starts Saturday night and by Sunday afternoon (in the argot of the times) he's boiled, blistered, snockered, loaded, organized and lit up, and the other Pooles all hate him. There's a lot of yelling then, swearing and things banging around inside the old house, following which, predictable as the tides, Barney throws Gail out of the house, then Marlin—not literally but he pushes them out the front door and across the sagging porch while swearing, literally, they'll never set foot in the house again. There's more yelling and swearing then and things banging around inside the old house, following which old Mrs. Poole, technically speaking, throws Barony out—shoves him out the door and across the sagging porch while screaming he'll never set foot in the house again and, if it's a really good fight, throwing stuff at him: his empty bottle, shoes, his overalls, a kerosene lamp once, a big frying-pan another time.

Hinty was a little late with his hot news flash. Gail and Marlin are already out in the yard when the kids peer through the cornstalks. Gail's in the hammock she spends a lot of time in, her skirt halfway up her legs, reading a Photo Fan Magazine. Gail's a waitress on and off in

Old Tim's Estate

Winatchee Falls but currently at liberty. Marlin's doing one-arm pull-ups on an old swing set, the swing long gone like the former Mrs. Barney Poole, another Burns girl with extremely bad judgment in men. There's some yelling and swearing but not much banging around inside the old house, then old Mrs. Poole, she's up in her eighties, ejects Barney, shoves him out the door and across the porch and shakes her old fist at him but doesn't throw anything at him. Barney snarls at his offspring, who ignore him, and weaves across the yard, bound for the poolhall. Gail and Marlin go back in the house and all's quiet on the Poole front. Barney and Marlin will be back at work on the Section Gang in the morning.

"Old lady Poole slowin' down," Hinty Murphy says, "she dint trun nuthin' at Barney. I seen them fight better. I seen Barney slapped Gail once, tell her pull her dress down. My brother Bert says Gail's a hot number."

Gail's legs, a hot number. Those, too, Eddie Devlin surmises, probably are springboards for the deadly Unclean Thoughts that Young Bernie Griffin who's studying to be a priest worries about a lot. But Eddie's not old enough (or wise enough, yet) to harbor or enjoy any deadly Unclean Thoughts. He wheels his bike out of the cornstalks, tells Petey walk home it's only a block and rides home himself. Father Coughlan, a priest who talks on the radio Sundays—rants and raves and howls actually about Social Justice, Ceil likes to listen to him—will be finished ranting and raving and howling and Eddie can fool around with the Atwater-Kent radio, maybe get Amos 'n Andy if he's lucky. Bee likes to listen to Amos 'n Andy. They're a funny pair of colored men—coons, but they're pretty funny, always in some kind of trouble they somehow get out of.

Eddie won't tell Ceil he watched the Pooles fight. Ceil can't stand the Pooles, thinks their public battles a "disgrace" and has on occasion called Gail a "tramp." The Pooles, Ceil says, ought to be a lesson to anybody who even thinks about drinking beer or wine or whiskey or anything. "The Pooles are the kind of people," she says, "Your grandfather spent his whole life trying to help." With little success, however. Help or else wipe from the face of the Earth, Eddie sometimes thinks. He once read a speech on the Evils of Drink and what should happen to drinkers—sort of read it anyway, it was an old newspaper clipping pasted in Bee's scrapbook—Old Tim Heaney gave when he was helping to make laws in the State Legislature.

Supper at the Devlins (Frank Pratt as usual absent, in Winatchee Falls with his mysterious lady friend) is cold chicken, stuffing and gravy, some tomatoes Bee canned which Eddie won't eat and the last of the apple pie. Estelle's not phoned again: there's been no further word regarding Timothy J. Heaney. The hopeful assumption is he's on his way to Omaha (or Chicago). He should have let Bergda know of course, but he might have tried to phone her, long-distance, and had phone trouble: that happens. Eddie overhears Ceil and Bee embracing this theory, actually Hack Devlin's theory.

Ernie Hoff, much to Ceil's disgust, shows everybody the leather helmet and goggles he bought mail-order for his first-flight and when stormbarning he goes, the loop-the-loop looping and rides giving, and lets Eddie try them on, though they're much too big for Eddie. "You'll break your neck in that silly airplane," Ceil says, but Ernie spoofs that prediction. He once an airplane already flew, he says. Not himself by exactly. Butch Doherty that used to fly the Air Mail and has his own airplane and fixes airplanes at the Winatchee Falls Airport and gave him four lessons at $4 each was in it, but he, Ernie, flew it. For a little while.

"Is easier than a car driving," Ernie says, "Nein clutch is there. Nein traffic. The feel of it pretty soon I got. Like a natural it at I am, Butch says." Then Ernie gathers up his helmet and goggles and up to bed goes, early to bed because tomorrow's a big day is, his first solo.

Eddie also goes early to bed, hustled off by Ceil with orders to say another prayer for Uncle Tim. It's a school night, she says, and he must be dead tired, up half the night last night, there are big circles under his eyes. Eddie can't detect these circles in the mirror in his

Old Tim's Estate

room but he is pretty tired. In fact, curled up in his cot, Uncle Tim briefly prayed for but his whereabouts no longer very exciting if he's only on a business trip to Omaha (or Chicago), Dare Devil Devlin is but halfway through his death-defying wing-walking act high above the jammed Grandstand at the Winatchee County Fairgrounds, everybody including Margie Bremer and Lorrie Stacowitz watching wide-eyed with their mouths wide open because Dare Devil Devlin is performing without a parachute—when he falls asleep.

4.

Monday morning. Bee rouses Eddie at eight a.m. Still groggy, he gets into his school clothes: clean bib overalls, a clean denim shirt and his old sneakers. There's been no further word, he inquires, regarding Timothy J. Heaney.

"We're pretty sure he went to Omaha," Bee says, "Or Chicago. To talk to one of those insurance companies. He might even be there by now. I'm sure Estelle will call when they hear from him."

Eddie discards, not without regret, his kidnap theory—Uncle Tim can work it out with Aunt Bergda, why he didn't phone her—and gulps his breakfast, Wheaties and a glass of milk. Eddie doesn't particularly like Wheaties, Breakfast of Champions though they be, but there's a coupon on the box he can send in with ten cents when the box is empty and get a Genuine Star Ranger Radio Ring with which to signal search aircraft should Trapper Devlin ever find himself stranded and facing starvation in the Great North Woods. Then it's off to school with the homework, the darned nine tables, he never got around to doing.

School starts at nine o'clock. The farm kids all have chores to do before they set out on foot for the schoolhouse built in 1892 on an acre on Stiles' southern edge designated for the purpose on George P. Stiles' original plat. It's a big white frame schoolhouse with two rooms, the Big Room and the Little Room, coat closets at the entrance to each, and a squat bell tower. It needs paint but its size is impressive:

Old Tim's Estate

most of the schools out in the country are one-room schools. Fractious students guilty (or suspected) of minor crimes are exiled to the coat closets, fifteen minutes to an hour depending on their crimes and previous criminal records. Serious crimes bring on a good whipping. A reliable eighth-grade boy thought likely to succeed in life rings the bell in the squat tower, pulling on a long rope in the Big Room coat closet at eight-fifty a.m., twelve-fifty p.m. and the end of the fifteen-minute recess that begins at ten a.m. Both rooms are in fact the same size but are called the Big Room and the Little Room because the big kids, grades five-eight, are in the Big Room and the little kids, grades one-four, are in the Little Room. Potbellied stoves heat both rooms but they've not been fired up yet, the weather still warm for this time of year. The split wood they burn is piled beside the double divided frame privy behind the schoolhouse. The District 14 School Board, Claude Clarke's the chairman, buys two cords every fall from Old Tom Ticke, more later if it's a long cold winter. The privy's divided by a wall separating the sexes but older boys with an abiding interest in the female form have cut peepholes in it. These peepholes are plugged with mud between observations so the teachers, both are females, won't spot them, but the teachers sometimes spot them all the same, in which case the usual suspects do time in the Big Room coat closet or, sometimes, get a good whipping.

There are thirty-nine students in the two rooms, twenty-two from Stiles, seventeen from the nine farms in District 14. There were forty but Augie Schlott quit school last week, the day he turned sixteen and legally could. His dad's laid up, a cow kicked him, and Augie's got to help with the farm work. He was going to quit anyway. There are only three eighth-graders left now and two, Vern Swenson and Morrie Riley, both farm kids, are counting the days until they're sixteen and considered educated. The other one is Bethany Hock, Alfred the farmer's daughter: her house is right across County Road S from the school, so she's never late. She gets straight As, plans to go to high school, Winatchee Falls High, take Commercial and become a private secretary. She can spell just about any word there is and placed third in the Winatchee County Rural Schools Spelling Bee last year, brought down by "algorithm," which she spelled with a "y" instead of an "i." She can spell it right now though and she's practicing for the next Spelling Bee, going through a dictionary and learning to spell words nobody ever heard of.

Miss Regina Mott, a thin spinster in her mid-thirties with flaming red hair and an overbite, twelve years in the Stiles trenches, teaches the Little Room. She wears sensible shoes and either of two brown dresses, one has a white collar, those the only garments her students have ever seen anyway. She rooms-and-boards as previously noted with the Boettchers—Joe Boettcher works at the Winatchee Falls chicken hatchery—but goes home to Predmore to see her folks weekends. The Boettcher kids, Ben in the fifth grade and Jerry in the third, detest this arrangement. Though quick with their little fists, they often are called "teacher's pets." Miss Mott almost stayed with the Devlins, Eddie moved into the parlor with Bee, and the Devlins could have used her $20 a month though it would have meant buying a bed, but Miss Mott decided it wouldn't "look right," her in a house with a single man, i.e., Ernie Hoff.

Miss Hilda Snodd, a big strong fearless woman in her fifties with iron-gray hair and a firm jaw, likewise a spinster, teachers have to be, eighteen years in the Stiles trenches, teaches the Big Room. Her wardrobe is more extensive than Miss Mott's and the Big Room girls often talk about her clothes. For all the boys care, she could wear armor or a hula skirt. Miss Snodd lives in Hayfield and drives to and from school every day in her 1924 Dodge coupe unless there's a blizzard or frost boils, in which case she stays with Miss Mott at the Boettchers. Miss Snodd, Eddie's heard, was (and presumably still is) an orphan. She came from somewhere Back East on an Orphan Train when she was about eleven and old Doc Snodd and his wife, who had no kids, adopted her. They were looking for cheap house help and whipped her a lot, so the story goes, but in the end after she went to the Winona Teachers College and became a teacher and they finally died she got their house.

Old Tim's Estate

Miss Snodd's also the school principal. Little Room malcontents Miss Mott can't handle, three-time losers in the coat closet, are sent to Miss Snodd in the Big Room for a good sound thrashing with a bamboo rod cut from the little end of a fishing-pole. Teachers can whip kids, that's a State Law and the consensus is that's the way it should be. These occasional thrashings, two or three a week usually, a dozen whacks or more laid on with enthusiasm the way old Doc Snodd laid them on, take place beside Miss Snodd's desk. The Big Room kids judge them as to duration, intensity and the stoicism displayed by the whipee and report on these later. The Little Room kids only hear the thwack the bamboo whacking a kid's butt makes and, sometimes, this kid crying. But the whippee on his return—red in the face, teary, much chastened—is thought to be and is in fact a lesson to all. Margie Bremer's the only Little Room girl ever sent to Miss Snodd, the day she called Clive Stoppel a "peckerhead" and hit him with a geography book, darn near putting his eye out. Margie took her dozen whacks without a whimper and said later her dad whacks her a lot harder with his belt.

But Margie's a notorious liar. Miss Snodd rates right up there with cyclones and Lenny Gibbons' fierce mad on the fear scale and when Eddie trots into the stchool yard—he seldom rides his bike to school because kids who don't have bikes always want to ride it—and finds Miss Snood inspecting the woodpile, he gives her a wide berth, then looks for kids he can tell the big news about the airplane's first flight. But all the Stiles kids and the farm kids too know that now. Margie Bremer, early to school, told them, stealing Eddie's thunder as the saying goes.

Vern Swenson, replacing Augie Schlott, is getting ready to ring the bell. Vern's success in life is problematical but he's a big kid, a big Swede, six feet tall, 170 pounds—his dad's 6-4 and weighs 280—and when Vern rings the bell you can hear it all over Stiles. Vern lets Eddie pull the bell-rope a couple of times: they're pals, sort of, despite the vast difference in their ages. Then Eddie joins the other kids reluctantly filing into the Little Room, hangs his jacket in the coat closet where everybody has a hook, and slides into his desk, the next to last one in the fourth-grade row, right behind Margie Bremer and in front of Buddy Douglas. Lorrie Stacowitz is in the fifth grade in the Big Room. She's pretty smart, skipped fourth-grade when she lived in Winona.

"Pledge of Allegiance," Miss Mott says, and everybody stands and pledges "allegiance to the Republic of Richard Strands." Then Eddie, seated, tackles the homework he didn't do. Eddie's a fair student but no whiz at arithmetic, the nine-tables and those beyond often stump him. Called on minutes later to rise and recite—Miss Mott's teacher's instinct targeting him—he runs aground at "nine times seven is sixty four," and Miss Mott tells him, Sit down and study your tables.

"Dummy!" Margie Bremer hisses. Eddie has no comment. He could dip Margie's dirty blonde pigtail in his inkwell, if she had a pigtail and he had an inkwell, like Tom Sawyer did to Becky Thatcher, but he'd likely get hit with a geography book. Margie, rubbing it in, stands and rattles off the nine-tables and Buddy Douglas sails through the ten-tables, but they're easier. The first and second grades stumble through Reading, the third grade struggles with the Names of the Great Lakes, all grades fill a page in their Palmer Method Workbooks with loops that look like the barbwire in front of the trenches in the Big War there was a picture of in The Weekly Reader, and an eon or so later it's finally time for the morning recess.

Morrie Riley and two seventh-grade boys, Ray Luck and Curly Diefendorfer, called Curly since Miss Snodd made his mother shave his head because he had nits, head for the outhouse and another advanced anatomy lesson, but most of the boys actually prefer an ongoing game they call Ay-rabs and Camels. Eddie, an Ay-rab, climbs on Vern Swenson's broad back, other small boys climb on bigger boys' backs and this desert battle begins, pair versus pair initially. This game began years ago, its inception lost to history, but it's a good game because just about everybody, big or small, can play it. Just about every boy, that is. Buddy Douglas doesn't play it much. He's too tall to be an Ay-rab and too skinny to be a Camel. Margie Bremer's asked to be an

Old Tim's Estate

Ay-rab but been turned down, naturally, because she's a girl, told go skip rope or something. The object of the game, it's a simple game, is to pull an Ay-rab off his Camel or, failing that, knock or topple this Camel and his Ay-rab to the ground. Vern and Eddie are the reigning champions, two-on-two, have been for weeks, that's why they're pals. The leading contenders are Hinty Murphy, his Ay-rab's Beanie Towey, a mean little third-grader, and Lionel Redhardt, a chunky farm kid in the seventh grade, one-eyed Petey Bremer's his Ay-rab.

Vern, using his great bulk, swiftly levels several Camels and their Ay-rabs and Eddie peels a few small Ay-rabs off their Camels, then, following a titanic struggle, peels Beanie off Hinty, though this too is mostly Vern's doing. Vern's got Eddie's legs in a vice-like grip and once Eddie gets an arm around Beanie's throat, uses Eddie like a tow-rope. Beanie complains, of course, cries foul, whines, "It ain't fair, Devlin, you was chokin' me!" Beanie's a poor loser. He climbs on Hinty's back again, convinces Lionel Redhardt and Petey Bremer and other Camels and their Ay-rabs, this usually happens, they should "gang-up" on Vern and Eddie and, following another titanic struggle, Vern and Eddie are hauled down, Eddie under Vern. But that's a pyrrhic victory. Two-on-two, Vern and Eddie are still the champions. Then Vern has to ring the recess bell. Eddie, somewhat bruised, threatens Beanie with bodily harm but backs off when Hinty intervenes and limps into the Little Room and another eon or so later it's noon, dinner time.

Eddie and the other Stiles kids go home for dinner. The farm kids bring lunches and eat in the schoolyard, sort of like a picnic every day, or at their desks in the winter or if it's raining out. Bee's got boiled potatoes, canned peas and a great platter of pork chops (Frank Pratt mopy or not will eat six or seven) on the table. There's been no further word regarding Timothy J. Heaney and Ernie Hoff has some devastating news.

"I Lenny's paster at look," Ernie says, "der ground too soft is dere to oop der airplane take. Al he tink so too. Vee vate better der ground hard freeze, hope no snow come. Den I oop der airplane take.

T.R. St. George

Tomorrow maybe." There's a cold snap on the way, predicted anyway, the low near fifteen degrees before morning: Ernie heard that on his radio at the lumberyard.

Hack Devlin shrugs. "It's your neck, Ernie," he says, and he's got that confounded Hupmobile to finish, the parts came this morning, delivered by the Tastee Bread truck. Ernie leaves for the lumberyard, Hack leaves for his garage, Frank Pratt spears another pork chop and Ceil tells Eddie he can't have a slice of the chocolate cake Bee baked until he eats all his peas.

"I think," Ceil also says, while Eddie eats his peas, swallowing them whole, "Ernie's getting cold feet. Him and his silly airplane!" But her heart's not really in this. She has another miserable headache, didn't sleep a wink, Timothy J. Heaney and all on her mind. She thinks Estelle should phone that insurance company in Omaha (or Chicago), what's one more long-distance call, make sure Tim's there and she's a mind to tell Estelle that. Bee says maybe Estelle did call. "She'd call us if she did and he was," Ceil says, "Do you think Estelle went in to work today?" Bee shrugs and Ceil decides she'll wait. Maybe Estelle will call. Ceil can't phone Estelle collect at S. Dolan & Sons except she's ordering a truckload of groceries and long-distance calls cost a pile of money.

Eddie leaves for school, full of news—Ernie's first flight postponed and he's the only kid knows that. He'll report the postponement, big disappointment though it is, be the center of attention for awhile, and wonders what he'll do after school, no first flight to witness. Bum around with Buddy Douglas probably, tell Buddy all about the expedition to Fairbow and how he held Young Charlie Goggins' police revolver, which he didn't get a chance to do Sunday, too darn many kids around and some of that's still a family secret except Buddy knows it. Run some MSP&P boxcars maybe. Take another look at the airplane-under-construction and hope, say a little prayer even, there's no snow and the cold snap freezes the ground in Lenny Gobbons' pasture really hard.

Old Tim's Estate

But these plans are temporarily delayed when another eon or so later Eddie comes home after school to put on his play clothes, old bib overalls and a sweater, it's turning colder, and finds Ceil in the kitchen reading a Winatchee Falls Bugle Call fresh off the press while Bee removes an apple pie from the cast iron stove. Banty Shanahan, after he picks up the Bugle Calls the MSP&P's three p.m. local drops off at the Depot, sometimes delivers the one the Devlins get, saving Bee a trip to the Post Office and cadging a piece of pie or something. Ceil likes to read the paper, soon as it comes, keep up with the news, read the obituaries, see who died, was there anybody they knew, and look for bargains in the ads, mainly clothes and grocery bargains. The Devlins and Bee buy most of their groceries once a week at the A&P or the Red Owl in Winatchee Falls, Claude Clarke's monopolistic prices, ten cents for a loaf of bread the A&P sells for eight cents, considered exorbitant. "Highway robbery," Ceil calls them.

Ceil finds a few bargains and runs them by Bee, the purchasing agent "Tittle Brothers have ham, nineteen cents a pound, and sausage, fourteen cents. Frank likes sausage once in awhile. So does Hack. Pork shank's nine cents." But the Devlins don't buy pork. They get pork free when Henry Heaney or Ed Devlin butcher a hog and give them a hind quarter. "Rubin's has oranges, two dozen for a quarter. A&P has coffee, three pounds for ninety-nine cents. That's kind of high. Bran Flakes, two packages for nineteen. Do you like Bran Flakes, Eddie?" Ceil flips a page. "Stevensons is having a sale, coats and dresses. Dresses at four-forty-nine. Fall coats at seven-ninety-five. But they'll all be Small or Extra Large. Sear's too, sheepskin coats, nine-ninety five to twelve-ninety-five. Hack could use a new coat. Overshoes, one-ninety-five. The Princess Cafe's advertising it's Special Thanksgiving Dinner already, dollar with all the trimmings—Oh my god! There's a story about Tim in the paper!"

T.R. St. George

FAMILY, FRIENDS CONCERNED

    Family and friends of Timothy J. Heaney, a well-known Winatchee Falls businessman, are concerned as to his present whereabouts. Mr. Heaney left for his office last Friday but did not arrive there and has not been seen since. He is thought to be on a business trip, the Bugle Call has learned, but there is concern since he apparently did not tell his office of his plans, as was his usual custom. Family and friends fear he may have taken ill somewhere. Mr. Heaney's business, Heaney Life Fire Casualty & Auto, is one of the leading insurance agencies in the city. He also is a director of the First National Bank.

A story about Tim in the paper!

118

Old Tim's Estate

It's not much of a story, in Eddie's opinion—Ceil reads it aloud, twice, then lets him have the newspaper—no hint in it Uncle Tim might been kidnapped, but Ceil's in an awful tizzy. "Oh God in Heaven!" she says or wails, "Everybody will know now! And the gossip will start! How'd the newspaper find out? I'm sure Estelle didn't say anything to anybody."

This mystery is soon solved. The phone rings, a long and three shorts, and Ceil answers it. "Estelle? Oh, yes, we just saw it! How? What? I can't hear you. Somebody's on the line." No matter though, now the story's out. "You think so? Tim should fire her! I mean, when he. You did? Bee thought you would. He wasn't? Oh my god, Estelle! I don't know either! Oh, we will. We are. I said a Rosary. We'll say another."

Ceil hangs up and, back in the kitchen, reports. "That was Estelle. She's at work. She's so mad she could spit! She said she didn't care if there were rubberneckers. It doesn't make any difference now anyway. She thinks it was Peggy Connell, Tim's office girl, spilled the beans. Told somebody Tim didn't come to his office Friday and the paper heard about it. One of those reporters at the newspaper called Estelle. She told him Tim was on a business trip. But he wrote that story anyway! Anything for a little news, I guess. Some sensation. You can't ever trust those reporters. I told Estelle, Tim should fire Peggy. When he. Estelle phoned that insurance company, the one in Omaha. Tim wasn't there. And the one in Chicago. He wasn't there either. There were people at both of them said they'd like to know where Tim is. Oh where is he? What's he doing? Oh I wish he'd stayed out of the Stock Market!"

Ceil's been reading newspaper stories about men who lost all their money when the Stock Market CRASHED and jumped from high windows, suicides, their immortal souls halfway Straight to Hell before the mess they made was scraped off the sidewalk. Eddie's still got his nose in the Bugle Call, headed for the sports page when he comes across a half-page ad reprinted, it says, with the permission of the Chicago Tribune.

T.R. St. George

ALL RIGHT, MISTER, NOW THE HEADACHE'S OVER!

For the last couple of weeks a good part of business in America has drifted away from the workbench to cock an excited eye at the biggest crap game the world has ever seen, the Stock Market. Well, that's that now and it's pretty well over except for the occasional bird who lost all his feathers and hurled himself from a high window. So let's not forget that millions upon millions of regular folks throughout this grand, greatly-desiring, gorgeously-spending America still need power, heat, light, food, transportation, recreation and adornment, same as always. If you're holding some good stocks at a loss, put 'em away and let 'em age—they'll be mellow and sweet a year or so from now. That's what Mr. John D. Rockefeller is doing. Business is not rotten. . . .

Eddie's faint interest in this fades. So what's to worry about? Mr. John D. Rockefeller is the skinny old guy with millions of dollars who gives away dimes there was a picture of giving some kid a dime in The Weekly Reader. Eddie says he thinks he'll go out and play—nobody seems to care, Ceil and Bee are reading the story about Tim again—and departs, gets his bike and rides to Al's Repair Shop.

Uncle Tim's back on the front-burner so to speak. Eddie revives his kidnapped theory. It's pretty well tattered though, no ransom note yet, and he reluctantly replaces it with the way many True Detective tales begin—with an unidentified body in the trunk of a car abandoned in a junkyard. But he really doesn't want to think about that. Not Uncle Tim. He takes a look at the airplane-under-construction. It looks the way it looked yesterday except Al's put instruments in the rear cockpit, fuel and oil pressure gauges and an ignition switch. Eddie inspects these: Al won't let him sit in the airplane. Buddy Douglas shows up on his new bike and they head for the boxcars on the MSP&P spur.

Old Tim's Estate

Buddy evinces no marked interest in Eddie's lengthy report on the expedition to Fairbow or Young Charlie Goggins' police revolver, and says, though he may be lying, he often fools around with the loaded 45-caliber automatic pistol his dad keeps in his desk in the Depot, case any mail thieves show up. They run a few boxcars and smoke, huddled in a smelly shed in the Stockyard, no open empty boxcars at hand and the weather much colder, two tailor-made Luckies Buddy filched from his dad's pack, then it's time for supper.

Supper at the Devlins is meat loaf, boiled potatoes and gravy, more peas and chocolate pudding. Ceil looks pretty grim at the table. Bee's subdued, sniffling a little. Hack's nursing a knuckle he skinned on Father Callahan's confounded Hupmobile. Frank Pratt's still mopy, though shoveling in the meat loaf, three helpings, and Ernie Hoff, catching the mood, he's not as "thick" as he's thought to be, has little to say beyond noting that, "It look like der hard freeze tonight vee get but no snow yet. So maybe t'morrow I der airplane oop take." If this news thrills anybody but Eddie, they don't show it.

Supper over, Ceil goes upstairs to lie down. Bee clears the table and starts washing the dishes. Frank and Ernie go off to the poolhall, where Ernie hopes to recruit a volunteer ground crew for his first flight. Hack puts a new mantle on the gasoline lamp and prepares some garage bills nobody will pay. Eddie does his homework, the hated eleven-tables, draws a few hated Fokkers going down in flames and goes to bed, nine o'clock on the dot, this no night to tangle with Ceil, instructed by Bee, "Say another little prayer your Uncle Tim's all right."

Curled up on his cot, two little prayers on the wires to Heaven ("Please God, make it so it freezes hard and keep Uncle Tim safe"), Eddie's plagued for a time by the unidentified body of a middle-aged man discovered in the trunk of a wrecked Buick in Sheeny's Junkyard on Winatchee Falls' far East Side. But Bulldog Devlin's not up to identifying this body or the party or parties responsible for its demise and soon drops off to sleep.

5.

Tuesday. Another endless half day of school slowly passes. Margie Bremer does thirty minutes in the Little Room coat closet, rifling the pockets in other kids' coat but finding nothing worth stealing. She called Clive Stoppel a "peckerhead" again and hit him with a ruler, just about taking his ear off. But Miss Mott thought Clive asked for that with a scurrilous remark regarding Margie's sister Sylvia and didn't send Margie to Miss Snodd for another whipping. Morrie Riley does an hour in the Big Room coat closet, warned he'll get a thrashing he'll "never forget" if ever Miss Snodd finds another peephole in the privy's dividing wall. Morrie's quoted as saying "old Snodd" will never see him again once he turns sixteen next week, though he'll let the air out of the tires on her old Dodge, he ever gets a chance. There is no Ay-rabs and Camels game. It's a bright sunny day but cold, the temperature around twenty, the ground frozen, too hard to fall on, and Vern Swenson's not in school, he's helping his dad fix fence or something. Miss Snodd rings the bell.

Eddie grabs a little limelight at recess, telling quit a few kids Ernie Hoff most likely will fly his airplane before the day is over. Some kids express doubt, but some farm kids say they'll delay their chores to watch that! Eddie's clearly thought to be the resident expert when it comes to the airplane, his dad after all rebuilt its engine, and basks in this celebrity. In fact, he's so excited by the prospect of the airplane's first flight he screws up the eleven tables when

Old Tim's Estate

called on after recess, going around at "eleven-times-ten is one-hundred-and-nine," and Margie Bremer calls him a "peckerhead."

Dinner at the Devlins—some kind of hot-dish Eddie doesn't relish, Bee's too worried to give it her best—is a dismal affair. It's been five days since Timothy J. Heaney went missing, no further word from Estelle. Bee's been crying, he eyes are all red. Ceil's clutching her Rosary, praying for Tim presumably. Hack's skinned knuckle is infected. Frank Pratt, usually rested and jolly on Tuesday, is subdued. Frank and his mysterious lady friend "broke up" Sunday night, Eddie hears Bee tell Hack, and tries to picture Frank and his lady friend, whoever she was, "broke up." All in pieces? Frank's still in one piece, subdued but shoveling in the hot-dish, three big helpings.

Ernie Hoff, usually a slow eater, gobbles up his hot-dish. "Al to see I got," he says, "Der airplane der shop from vee out poosh and der vings on put. Den it oop it take, I tink. Der ground enough is hard freeze. Tree-tirty maybe, I tink. After der vings vee on put and Lenny's paster it poosh." Skipping his desert, canned peaches, Ernie departs.

"You'll be there for that, I suppose?" Ceil, looking at Hack like she still was a teacher and he a fractious student, says. "Watching Ernie break his silly neck!"

"Just for a little while," Hack says, lying, "Just start the engine for him is all. I still got that confounded Hup to finish."

"Wasting more time!" Ceil says. But she really doesn't seem to care much one way or the other, what with Timothy J. Heaney and his whereaboyts and all on her mind, about Hack's time or Ernie's silly neck.

Eddie leaves most of his hot-dish, Ceil for once lodging no protest, likewise skips his canned peaches, scoots from the table, jumps on his bike and races to Al's Shop, arriving right behind Ernie. Eddie's the only kid present for awhile, the rest all eating dinner, and there's nobody else around, just a few dogs, Stiles generally is pretty somnolent during the dinner hour.

123

T.R. St. George

Eddie helps Al and Ernie, observed by the dogs, roll the airplane's fuselage out of the shop and across main street through the big gate into the lumberyard. Al's installed seatbelts, Eddie notes, wide canvas straps that clip to hooks in both cockpits. He'd help Al and Freddie carry the wings across the street too, but somehow the word—"They takin' Ernie's airplane out the shop!"—spreads and Banty Shanahan, Poop Clarke, Lee J. Lilly and half a dozen kids turn up. Likewise Hack Devlin. The kids soon get in the way and Ernie orders them, even Eddie, "Back from der airplane vings avay stand!" Hack, Poop, Banty, Lee J. Lilly and Ernie carry the wings across the street and the kids, then, watch from the lumberyard gate while Ernie hops around giving bad advice and Banty, Poop and Lee J. Lilly slide the lower wing through a big slot in the bottom of the fuselage between the cockpits. Al and Hack bolt this wing tight to the fuselage. Lenny Gibbons turns up and helps Poop and Banty and Lee J. Lilly pick up the top wing and hold it in place while Al and Hack connect it to the bottom wing with a dozen struts and numerous wires they pull taut. Claude Clarke comes over from his store, keeping an eye on it, and gives it as his opinion they should sell tickets for the first flight: but it's too late for that now. A farmer seeking three rolls of tarpaper shows up and Ernie, though irritated, goes to get the tarpaper.

Eddie ducks into the lumberyard and asks Hack, "When it be ready to fly?"

"Couple hours prolly," Hack says, "We still have to check the controls. Make sure they're hooked up okay. Don't bother us now."

Eddie jumps on his bike, the school bell's ringing, and races to school, beating all the other kids present with this exclusive hot news flash. "Ernie Hoff's gonna fly his airplane this afternoon! For sure! Round three-thirty! In Lenny Gibbons' pasture! I help roll it out Al's shop!"

He tells Miss Mott this too. She tells Miss Snodd and Miss Snodd—this an all-school announcement and a first—says school will let out ten minutes early so those students who wish to may watch the airplane make its first flight. "May," Miss Snodd notes, shoving in a little

Old Tim's Estate

grammar, being the proper "permissive term" in this case since they all have eyes (though Petey Bremer has only one that works) and are "capable" of watching the airplane's first flight.

Three-twenty comes a couple of weeks later.

All thirty-eight students, even the girls, race through Stiles still in their school clothes, Eddie on his bike, and join the crowd already assembled in a loose half circle around the airplane at the top of the slope in Lenny Gibbons' pasture, everybody gawking at the airplane and trying not to step in the fresh and half-frozen cowpies underfoot. It's a bright sunny afternoon, still chilly, a light breeze blowing. Eddie surveys the crowd. It looks like most of Stiles' ambulatory population and more. The Section Gang is there, its puddle-jumper parked on the spur. So is old Mrs. Gibbons, all bundled up in her wheelchair, bumped across the MSP&P tracks and through the broken pasture gate by her daughter Luverne. Claude Clarke, of course, looking important—he put a sign on the door at the store, Poop Clarke says, Closed Until After The Airplane Flys. Vern Swenson and his dad, all 280 pounds of him: they somehow got the word and came in their old truck. Frank Pratt, the poolhall also temporarily closed. Banty Shanahan, the volunteer ground crew Ernie enlisted, looking official in his old A.E.F. jacket with the dog-collar and brass buttons, which he wears on special occasions. A few farmers and their wives and some younger offspring waiting for Claude Clarke's store to open. Whip Rahilly and Slicky Riordan, Slicky's Harley parked behind the lumberyard, how they got the word a mystery but no matter. They skipped their last class at Winatchee Falls High, Whip tells Eddie, so's not to miss the airplane's first flight.

Miss Snodd and Miss Mott arrive in Miss Snodd's old Dodge coupe, park beside the Harley and watch the excitement from there.

"Your dad and Al and Ernie and Banty there and Poop and Frank," Whip also tells Eddie, "they had a hell of a time gettin' the airplane out the lumberyard and inna the pasture on account of the wings are wider'n the gates. You dad, he finally figger it out. He figger if they sort of cant it sideways like they could get it through the gates and they did."

Eddie's pretty proud of Hack, given this information: it sounds like Hack might of saved the day. Margie Bremer's edged close to the airplane to watch Hack's tinker with the engine. Al's tinkering with the control wires and Banty's caressing the propeller. Eddie joins Margie, but Ernie promptly pounces on them.

"Nein! Nein!" Ernie yells, "Avay the airplane back from stand!" Ernie's wearing his new sheepskin coat and leather helmet and goggles, the goggles pushed up, and he's hopping around and puffing with excitement. Whip Rahilly says Ernie's been yelling at the crowd, "Avay the airplane back from stand!" since it was canted through the pasture gate, afraid somebody will touch it while Hack and Al tinker with it.

Margie and Eddie retreat and stand beside Claude Clarke, Claude always find a good place to stand at local events, at which point Lenny Gibbons arrives looking pleased accompanied by a stranger, a medium-sized man with a bony face wearing a suit, a vest draped with a watch chain, a hat and a dark overcoat.

"Claude," Lenny says, "like you t'meet Mister Allen here. Mister Webster R. Allen. Mister Allen, he's the lawyer the railroad sent. He come and settle with me for that prize cow mine was kilt the time the freight hit her."

Claude Clarke and Mr. Allen shake hands. "Mister Gibbons here," Mr. Allen says, "drives a hard bargain. But our policy, the Milwaukee St. Paul and Pacific Railroad, is we always make a fair settlement, any livestock our trains injure or destroy. Mister Gibbons also convinced me I should come and see this airplane fly. Airplane built right here in uh Stiles, I believe—"

"That's right," Claude Clarke, looking important, says. "Built right here in Stiles. Locally. By three our residents. That's quite a thing, you know, build an airplane. We got some pretty smart people here. I believe it be taking off any minute now."

Old Tim's Estate

"Well I hope I can see that," Mr. Allen, pulling a big gold watch from his vest pocket, says. "I have to catch the four-eighteen to Milwaukee though—"

"You ever been up in uh airplane, Mister?" Banty Shanahan, quick to join any conversation and at loose ends while Hack and Al tinker with the airplane, says.

"Well, no, I haven't." Mr. Allen says, "I'd like to go up in one but I haven't had that opportunity." He surveys Ernie's airplane. "You know, this airplane looks a little bit like, I can't member the name but I think it was an observation plane. In The War—"

"Sopwith-Camel prolly," Banty says, "What the Limey's called them. Was you in The War, Mister? In France—"

"No," Mr. Allen says, "Not in France. I was in the Army for awhile. But I only got as far as Camp Grant, Illinois. Then The War was over and I went back to college—"

"Yeah, well, you dint miss much, some ways," Banty says. "You ever get a chanct though, go up in uh airplane, you should. I was a flier awhile. In The War. In France—Hey! Look like we're about ready t'go here!"

Hack Devlin's done fiddling with the engine. "She's ready," he says. Al Morris slides from under the airplane, confers with Hack and concurs and the crowd, which was getting somewhat restless, stirs. So do Lenny Gibbons' fierce mad bull and Holsteins, huddled near the old barn at the foot of the slope in the pasture. They've been eyeing the crowd and the airplane (another monster dragonfly) with what appears to be suspicion, though it's hard to tell about that with Holsteins.

"Okay, Lindbergh," Al tells Ernie, "Climb in!"

Ernie gulps and swallows, his mouth may be a little dry. Al gives him a boost and, grunting, Ernie gets up into and settles in the airplane's rear cockpit. He pulls his goggles down over his eyes. Eddie's so excited he darn near pees in his pants and two little kids, farm kids, do, then stand around shivering in their wet pants, nobody, not even their mothers, paying them any attention, everybody gawking at

T.R. St. George

Freddie and the airplane like they never saw one before, which maybe some never did, not up close like this anyway.

Banty Shanahan twists the propeller, cranking it up. "Contact!" Ernie says, his voice sort of squeaky, and flips the ignition switch, and the crowd draws a long collective expectant breath. Banty heaves on the propeller. The engine starts, Hack Devlin guaranteed it would, coughs and sputters, then rattles away. The propeller's a spinning blur and the airplane's shaking like it's ready to fall apart but it's not moving.

"The blocks!" Hack hollers, "Wheels still blocked!" The blocks are oak chunks Al made, tied to ten-foot ropes. Hack ducks under the port wing and grabs one rope, Whip Rahilly ducks under the starboard wing and grabs the other. They pull the blocks—

And the airplane lunges forward, yaws, straightens, rolls down the pasture slope, splashing through cowpies, gains speed and lifts from the ground! Accompanied by ragged cheer. It's airborne for maybe twenty feet, achieving an altitude of four or possibly six feet, witnesses later disagree—then dives, burying its nose in the pasture turf. The propeller shatters, pieces flying every which way. The wheels come off. The wings crumple. The tail swings up. The engine snarls and dies. Likewise the cheer. And Ernie, he forget to fasten his seatbelt, (1) ejects from the rear cockpit like The Great Stromboli The Human Cannonball ejected from his cannon (Two Performances Daily) at the Winatchee County Fair, (2) performs like The Great Stromboli a half somersault in midair and (3) lands with an audible whomp! on his back on the pasture turf in a half-frozen (or half-thawed) cowpie. The Great Stromboli landed in a net and was up on his feet in an instant, waving to the crowd in the Granstand. Ernie Hoff lies motionless, not even a twitch. And Lenny Gibbons' fierce mad bull and Holsteins, spooked by all this, stampede, bawling, and scatter to the far end of the pasture.

Old Tim's Estate

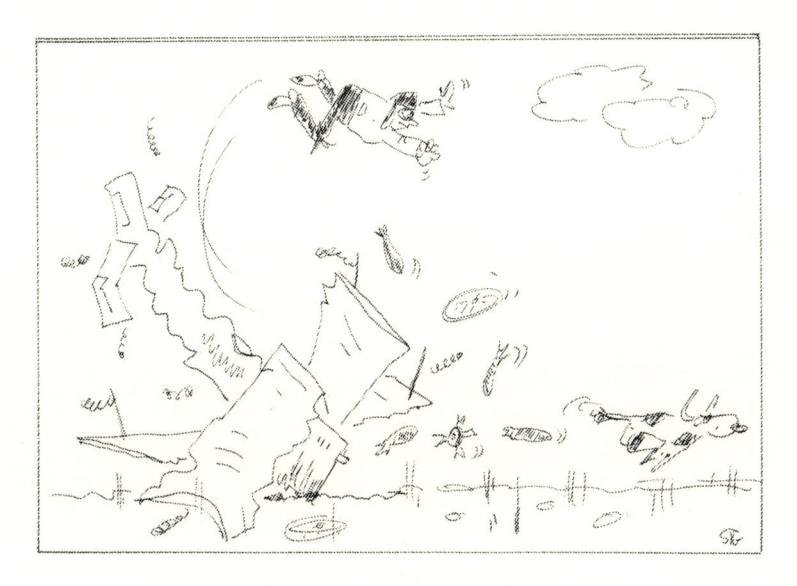

Ernie ejects from the airplane.

"No! Wait! Stay back!" Hack Devlin hollers as the spectators surge forward but he might as well holler at the wind. All the spectators including Mr. Allen, holding his hat, his overcoat flapping, and old Mrs. Gibbons in her wheelchair pushed along by Luverne race down the slope by the wrecked airplane and mill around Ernie's prone body, which shows no signs of life.

"Stand back! Don't move him!" Claude Clark, pushing a couple of kids aside, says. "He may have suffered injuries! Internal injuries—"

"I've had First Aid," Mr. Allen, kneeling beside Ernie, says—kneeling in a fresh cowpie, he discovers later. He finds Ernie's wrist and Ernie's pulse, which is racing, clocking around 150, and Ernie opens his eyes, he's still wearing his goggles, blinks, gasps, the wind pretty well knocked out of him, and gurgles.

"Happen vot?" Ernie gurgles.

It's a miracle, more or less, but Ernie's not injured, internally or otherwise, nothing broken anyway, just bruised, his sheepskin coat soaked up most of the impact when he hit the turf. He's badly shaken though, no wonder, and his sheepskin coat's a mess, slathered with cowpie. Mr. Allen, Claude Clarke and Banty gingerly help Ernie stand up. He gets his wind back. His back hurt is, he says, or moans, and he whacked both his knees, tearing his corduroy pants, when ejected from the airplane. He's still dazed. He surveys the wrecked airplane, what's left of it, a dream shattered like the propeller "Oop vas," he says, "Den happen vot?"

"It nosed over," Al Morris says, "Dived. But you're right, Ernie. It was up! It flew! It was off the ground! It was in the air! We'll check the controls. I can make another propeller. We'll fix it up and try again—"

"Nein! I no tink," Ernie says, "Or it you oop it take, Al." He removes his goggles. "Vot smell is?" It's his sheepskin coat, splattered with cowpie. "Oh sheet! All over wit cowsheet my coat is! Off it take help me. A bat I am need!" Lenny Gibbons, he's used to cowsheet, helps Ernie out of his reeking coat, holds it at arm's length and wonders what should he do with it? Ernie thinks a minute: that coat cost $9.95 on sale at Sears. "By der lummeryard put. Der hose vit I varsh." He takes another look at his shattered dream. Then, bent double, moaning, rubbing his back and banged-up knees, assisted by Milo Stacowitz and Franz Geist, trained medics in view of the many minor injuries suffered by the Section Gang, he limps up the slope to the pasture gate. Ernie's dream now is a washtub full of near-scalding water in the little room off the Devlin's kitchen, Bee will heat the water, in which to clean himself up and soak his bruises. Ernie usually bathes Saturday night but this is an emergency.

Hack Devlin, Al Morris and the spectators inspect the wrecked airplane while exchanging various versions of its brief flight and abrupt disaster, then, the excitement over, the spectators but for the small boys and Margie Bremer slowly depart. Claude Clarke leaves to open his store. Frank Pratt says he'll be opening the poolhall.

"Ernie better thank his lucky stars," Banty Shanahan says, "Most all the airplanes I seen crashed in The War in France, they catch fire soon's they hit the ground and burn up like a bonfire and burn everbody was in them crispy."

"You tell me that now," Mr. Allen, dabbing at the cowsheet on his overcoat with a handful of grass, says. "I think I'll just wait awhile before I go up in an airplane." Giving up with the grass, he looks at his watch, says it's time he got to the depot to catch the four-eighteen to Milwaukee, shakes hands with Lenny Gibbons and departs, picking his way along the Main Line track, walking on the ties.

"He's a pretty good fella, that lawyer, for a lawyer," Lenny tells Lee J. Lilly and Banty.. "Or elst he don't much about cows. Thirty-two dollars he give me finally for my old cow was kilt! Old cow wasn't worth but eighteen. I screw the railroad!"

Lee J. Lilly and Banty evince little interest in this. They're arguing about their $2 bet, Banty claiming the airplane "flew" and he won, Lee J. Lilly contending it did not "really fly, didn't fly any where anyway," and he won.

The small boys and Margie Bremer inspect the wrecked airplane further. Its brief flight and crash and Ernie ejecting from the cockpit was pretty exciting but a big disappointment too. All the mean scruffy kids in hated Simpson, Judgment and Predmore, some come to Mass at Precious Blood, will no doubt laugh like hyenas when they hear the story of this air disaster and the really dumb scruffy Simpson kids will retain most of the bragging rights. There's a dance hall in Simpson called the Rainbow Ballroom, open weekends, and Simpson kids get to watch the fights in its parking lot, half a dozen fights some Saturday nights. Poop Clarke and Marlin Poole often go there and Marlin usually gets into a fight, sometimes two or three—

"I knew it wouldn't fly," Buddy Douglas says. "My Dad bet it wouldn't—"

"It flew!" Eddie says, defending Hack Devlin's part in the Great Experiment. "It was up in the air! You must had your eyes shut!"

"I seen it fly," Margie Bremer says, and Eddie could almost hug her.

"You call that flyin'?" Buddy says, or sneers. "I can trun a ball farther it was up the air!"

T.R. St. George

"Baloney you can!" Eddie says, and turning his back on Buddy joins Hack and Al Morris beside the wreckage. "Baloney" is not a very devastating rejoinder but the best Eddie can manage. He feels sorry for his Dad, all the hours Hack spent working on the airplane's engine and the airplane really didn't fly—didn't fly much anyway. Ceil no doubt will have plenty to say about that and she'll say it about a hundred times. But the engine ran good, made a lot of noise, spun the propeller. It's not his Dad's fault the airplane really didn't fly.

"I'll haul it back the shop," Al Morris says. "See I can figger out what went wrong. It look to me like it was going to fly. It took-off good. Then something went wrong and blooey! I wonder it was Ernie did something dumb? But it really ain't smash up all that bad. I can fix it up. Make a new propeller and we'll try it again—"

"You better take some flying lessons then," Hack says. "You heard Ernie. It ain't him going up in it again. I think Ernie's flying days are over. He won't be doing any barnstorming or loop-the-loops looping or rides giving. Doubt we'll ever see any the money he owes us either Way it goes, I guess."

Dare Devil Devlin, overhearing this, has a bright idea. He could take a few flying lessons and fly the airplane! When it's fixed. But $4 a lesson! That's another figure like the National Debt. Besides, Ceil will never let him, afraid he'll get killed. Thus another brief exciting dream dies and so, it turns out, does Ernie Hoff's hot bath dream. He encounters Bee Heaney in her old winter coat and overshoes at the pasture's broken gate.

"Is Hack here?" Bee says, "What happened to the airplane?"

"It oop went den down," Ernie says. "By vot left is Hack is. I am a bat need—"

But Bee's through the broken gate, calling, "Hack! Hack! Come here! I have to talk to you! Right away!" Hack and Eddie leave the wrecked airplane and join Bee. She's been crying, her eyes are all red. "They found Tim! Estelle called. He's in Albuquerque! With Edna. Estelle talked to him. It sounds like he lost a lot of money in the Stock Market! Near as Ceil could tell. Estelle's pretty upset. Lost a lot

Old Tim's Estate

of money and I guess that was too much for him and he just lit out!" Bee starts crying. "Oh, Hack! Estelle said something about our house! I'm not sure what. Estelle's pretty rattled, I guess. She said damn the rubberneckers and didn't make a whole lot of sense, Ceil says. But you better come home, Hack. Right away! Ceil's taking it awful hard!"

6.

Timothy J. Heaney returns to Winatchee Falls on Sunday, November 17, on a Greyhound bus, arriving at eight p.m. Edna buys his ticket and phones with his schedule and Bergda and Estelle meet him and take him home to West College Street in a taxi. Tim's just about done in. He takes a long hot soaking bath and falls into bed. He rode the last four-hundred miles from Omaha beside an unemployed oil field roustabout who weighed about three hundred pound and, this Tim's estimate, had not had a bath since Flag Day (June 14).

Somebody sees Tim arrive and tells somebody who tells somebody and the reporter at the Bugle Call calls Estelle at work Monday for what he calls "a follow-up on the Heaney story." Estelle, pretty snippety, tells this reporter, "Mind your own business, my father was on a business trip" and, there being nothing very sensational in that, there is no follow-up in the Bugle Call.

All the Heaneys, however, over the next couple of days, conducting their own follow-up, run up some long-distance phone bills, titillating many rubberneckers but this is a family crisis, rubberneckers be dammed, and on Wednesday not-so-snippety Estelle phones everybody, the whole clan—Ceil and Hack Devlin and Bee, Gert and Old Charlie Goggins, Nell and Wesley L. Kemp, Henry Heaney and Emma—and asks them to come and "have a little talk with Tim." Eight p.m. Saturday in his fancy house on West College Street.

Old Tim's Estate

"To get all the bad news, I guess," Ceil says, while they chug along in the Model T on their way to Winatchee Falls, Eddie in the backseat with Bee because there's nobody Ceil trusts to leave him with. "Our brother's sad story, whatever it is."

Timothy J. Heaney's slumped in one of the big overstuffed chairs in his living room when the Devlins and Bee arrive. Everybody else is there already, sitting around on the big couch, in the other big chair and on some dining room chairs, their coats draped here and there, all looking like this is some dead person's wake. Young Charlie Goggins, his 220 pounds on a dining room chair he may crush at any moment, brought Gert and Old Charlie in Tim's Buick: they'll go home with Nell and Wesley L. Kemp in Wesley's new Studebaker President. Henry and Emma Heaney left Little Tim and his baby sister with Emma's mother.

Timothy J. Heaney looks older if no wiser, thinner, though he's got a little color in his cheeks, pink. He spent some afternoons in Albuquerque, it comes out, in a deck chair on Edna's patio, the sky overcast, but the New Mexico sun drilled him right through the clouds. He's wearing the pants to one of his suits and a shirt but no collar or tie and he's twisting his hands like he's washing them without any soap or water. He needs a shave and the gray hair over his ears is ragged He needs a haircut and doesn't remember it soon will be Eddie's tenth birthday, December 7—doesn't wish Eddie a happy birthday anyway or slip him a dollar—though rising to greet Ceil and Hack and Bee and mumbling it's good of them to come.

Estelle for once isn't chattering like a squirrel. She looks like she's been crying a lot and her permanent's collapsed. Bergda greets Bee and the Devlins with muted enthusiasm, she looks like she's been crying for about a month, then sits on the arm on Tim's chair and smoothes his ragged hair. Ceil orders Eddie into the kitchen, where Edith's taking an angel food cake out of the oven. Edith's been crying too, her eyes are all red and puffy, but remembers it soon will be Eddie's birthday.

"It won't be a very happy birthday, I guess," Edith says, "What with

T.R. St. George

Timothy J. Heaney and his wife Bergda, observed with distaste by Old Tim Heaney when a State Representative, confront the Heaney clan.

Dad and all." Then, sniffling, she ladles coffee into the electric percolator.

"Oh, I don't know," Eddie says. He's heard or overheard, his Uncle Tim apparently did a terrible thing, but doesn't know what this thing is. And Bee will bake a chocolate cake for his birthday, Ceil will let

Old Tim's Estate

him eat two pieces after he blows out the candles and he's pretty sure he'll get red fender reflectors for his bike and some new mittens. He was hoping for more but Ceil's said about a thousand times when she wasn't crying they have to "watch our pennies now."

Edith gives Eddie a cookie, it's pretty stale, and he edges close to the kitchen door to eavesdrop on the desultory conversation in the living room, which briefly concerns the weather, still warm for this time of year after the cold snap, no snow yet in the forecast. But that subject's soon exhausted. It's followed by a long silence, which lasts until Timothy J. Heaney coughs and clears his throat and says, "Well, I guess you all want to know what happened."

"Yes," Ceil says, "I think we do. I think we should know. You want to know, don't you, Nell? Gert? Henry? Bee?"

The siblings all mutter and murmur assent and Timothy J. Heaney clears his throat again like he's got one of those frogs in it. "Well," he says, " I stayed in the Stock Market a little bit too long. Took my broker's advice. Bad advice. I was just about ready to sell all my stocks, take a nice profit and get out of the Market. Then the damn Market CRASHED. Black Thursday, they're calling it now. Stocks started going through the floor. But I guess you all know that. Anyway, I had to boost my margins and boost them again and I had some broker loans. I plain ran out of cash. The fact is, I got cleaned out. I lost everything. All my stocks. All my money. Everything. That's what happened—"

"What do you mean," Ceil says, "everything?"

Timothy J. Heaney clears his throat and sort of hems and haws. "Well, um," he hems and haws, "I mean everything, Ceil. This house, most likely. I took out a second mortgage and invested that money in the Stock Market. And your house, Ceil, your house and Bee's, I'm sorry to say. I took out a little mortgage on your house, three-thousand dollars, and invested that money in the Stock Market. And lost it. Week before the CRASH, you know, I was worth close to one-hundred-thousand-dollars! I mean my stocks were. I bought some Cities Service at fifty-six and it went to one-hundred-and-forty-nine. I bought some General Motors at forty-four and it went to one-hundred-and-twenty-eight. I bought some Blue Ridge Investments at thirty-seven and it went—"

"Our house!" Ceil, stunned for a moment, says, shrieks actually, "You lost our house! Oh my God, Tim!" Ceil when a child heard many tales about the poor Irish evicted by cruel British landlords during the Great Potato Famine, ordered off their tenant holdings and left to starve on the roads and in the ditches. No place to live: that's a grim ethnic memory.

There's another long silence while Timothy J. Heaney sighs like he might be running out of air, then says, "Your house isn't lost, Ceil. It's just mortgaged, is all. Twenty-year mortgage at six per cent. Don't worry—"

"Don't worry!" Ceil says, or shrieks. "Are you crazy, Tim! Where'd you get all that money anyway? Buy all those stocks? Think you were J.P. Morgan."

There's another long silence, then Timothy J. Heaney sighs again like he's just about ready to give up and die. "I took money from The Estate. I cashed in those railroad bonds and invested that money in the Stock Market. I though Estelle explained all that—"

"Maybe she did," Ceil says, "But Estlle wasn't making much sense, she talked to me. I think we should hear it from you, brother Tim. Everything you did! That we didn't know you were doing! We might's well get all the bad news."

There's another long silence then Timothy J. Heaney sighs again like he's just about ready to give up etc. "I just told you, Ceil. I cashed in the railroad bonds and I invested that fifteen-thousand in the Stock Market. I bought some more Cities Service and more Blue Ridge and. . . . Well, I guess that doesn't matter much now. The Estate, though. The Estate was worth close to forty-thousand dollars when the damn Market—"

"How much," Nell Kemp, sticking her oar in, says, "is it worth now?"

Timothy J. Heaney sighs again like etc. "There isn't any Estate any more, Nell. It's gone. All gone. I thought Estelle told Ceil—"

Old Tim's Estate

"Oh my God!" Ceil says or sobs while her siblings babble, "We're all poor then! We'll always be poor now! Oh damn you, Tim! I don't remember what Estelle said. I was too upset. But you took money out of The Estate! That was our money! Supposed to be. And you mortgaged our house! Oh, Tim! You know the way Dad felt about mortgages! What's going to happen to us now? Where will we live—"

"Oh for god's sake," Timothy J. Heaney, exhibiting signs of life, says, "You can still live in the house, Ceil. Assume the mortgage. Twenty dollars a month, about, be the mortgage payment. I'll work it all out with the First National Bank. Once Arnold Felke's back on his feet. I'm not the only one this happened to, you know. There wasn't anything in the newspaper, but Arnold, president the First National, lost more than I did. Arnold tried to commit suicide. With his shotgun. He missed but sort of scalped himself. He's in the Community Hospital. In a straight jacket. And I'll help you out with the mortgage payments. Once I get back on my feet. It's not the end of the world, Ceil—"

"The hell it's not!" Ceil says, swearing in Eddie's near presence but she's pretty wrought up. "Where are we going to get twenty dollars a month for a mortgage payment for a house that was ours! Supposed to be ours, long as we lived! While you get back on your feet. Besides there's The Estate. Was The Estate! Damn you, Tim! Your took our money! You stole our money! What happens now, somebody gets sick?"

Timothy J. Heaney can't answer that question, apparently. He doesn't say anything anyway, but Bergda speaks up. "Tim wasn't stealing! He was investing! He didn't do it, lose a lot of money, on purpose! He didn't know the Stock Market was going to CRASH. Nobody did. And now we might lose our house—"

So?" Ceil says, "Tim lost our house! Good as—"

"Charlie here," Gert Goggins, putting her oar in, says, "Doctor says he's got a hernia, needs a hernia operation. He'd like to go to Mayo Brothers, get it done right. We were counting on The Estate, you know, pay for that. Like Dad's Will said. What about that, Tim?"

Timothy J. Heaney can't answer that question either, but Hack

139

Devlin the eternal optimist has a thought. "Well, whatever. You still got your insurance business, Tim. Office and all—"

"No, Hack," Timothy J. Heaney, sighing again like etc., says, "I'm afraid not. I used some premiums I had in escrow to boost my margins when some of my stocks took a dive. So I could stay in the Market till they went up again. Try to, I mean." This is not exactly news to everybody but it's a minor part of the general disaster: nobody comments. "Those insurance companies want that money now. That's another little problem I have. And they already revoked my agreements, contracts, I was their agent. My insurance business is closed. I let Peggy Connell and Young Matt Malloy go Wednesday. Phoned them from Edna's. And the word will get around, the industry. You can bet on that. I doubt I'll be selling any more insurance, Hack—"

"Serves Peggy right!" Estelle says, "Blabbermouth Connell—"

"And what about Young Charlie here," Gert, putting another oar in, says. "He got that parking ticket was on you car fixed and paid the tow charge, two dollars, get your car out the Impound Lot, and put a dollar's worth gas in it, drive us over here. That's three dollars he's got invested in your Buick! And Yegga and him have another baby coming—"

"Estelle," Timothy J. Heaney, with another long sigh etc., says, "Could you—"

"Oh sure, Dad," Estelle says, and hops up and goes into the dining room and comes back with her purse, digs into it and gives Gert three dollars bills.

"Thank you," Gert says. And for the first time perhaps the rest of the Heaney clan grasp the full awful devastating disaster the Stock Market CRASH was. Timothy J. Heaney, a man who liked to walk around with fifty or sixty dollars in his wallet has to ask his daughter for three dollars! But if this triggers any clan sympathy it's easily suppressed.

"Albuquerque," Ceil says, "that's another thing! What in the world was the big idea, taking off for Albuquerque without telling anybody? You know what you put all of us through—"

"Tim was under a lot of stress," Bergda says. Bergda, Eddie learns,

Old Tim's Estate

flayed Tim to a fare-the-well in private. "My folks," Edith says, "had an awful fight." But confronting the hostile clan now, Bergda's supportive.

"So tell us, then," Ceil says, "about your little trip."

"Well I was under a lot of stress," Timothy J. Heaney, with another long sigh etc., says. "The Stock Market CRASHED. My Cities Service went to twenty-four. My General Motors went to nineteen. My Blue Ridge.... Well, whatever. My broker was after me, boost my margins again. Those insurance companies I owed premiums, they were after me. I guess I wasn't thinking real straight. But what I thought, I thought Warren, Edna's husband, he just bought the Nash dealership in Albuquerque, might help me out. Loan me some money. Temporarily. Just so I could boost my margins and hold on to my stocks. But you can't just phone somebody, even they're related, and ask them, loan you quite a lot of money. You have to talk to them. Personally. So I started out that Friday morning, sort of on the spur of the moment, to drive out to Albuquerque and talk to Warren. But I got as far as Fairbow, I realized I couldn't drive all the way out to Albuquerque. Fifteen-hundred miles. I just wasn't up to it, stress I was under and all. So I decided to stop, get a hotel room, think was there some other way out of the bind I was. I should have phoned Bergda then, not worry anybody, but—"

"It's all right, dear," Bergda says, smoothing Timothy J. Heaney's ragged gray hair. "You were under a lot of stress. But it's all over now—"

"I didn't have very much cash with me either," Timothy J. Heaney says, "I had all I had but that wasn't very much. I didn't have any luggage either, check-in a hotel. I tried to swipe a suitcase at the Bus Depot but the woman owned it caught me. I told her I mistake it was mine and got out there. I bought a cheap suitcase and got a room in a lousy hotel. And I thought and I thought all the rest that day and all night. I didn't sleep at all hardly. But the only thing I could think of was borrow some money from Warren, boost my margins again, hold onto my stocks or some of them anyway and wait'll they went up again. That's what John D. Rockefeller's doing, you know. I ducked out the lousy hotel in the morning. Didn't pay my bill. Edna paid it. Sent the hotel a check. I couldn't write a check, it would've bounced. And I took a bus to Albuquerque. It left around noon and I had just about enough cash for the bus ticket. I didn't get off the bus all the way to Albuquerque, except go to the bathroom at the rest stops and change buses in Kansas City. And I didn't eat anything. No meals, I mean. I only had two dollars. I ate some candy bars."

This sad tale does not elicit any apparent clan sympathy either. It's followed by a long silence broken by Wesley L. Kemp, a fat little man with a fat face and long sideburns, no diplomat he, who says, "Y'know, I made a few dollars in the Stock Mar—"

"Oh, shut up!" Nell, his wife, says. "Nobody want to hear another dammed word about the Stock Market!" Wesley L. Kemp shuts up.

"So now you're in Albuquerque," Ceil says, "Sunning yourself on Edna's patio while we're all worried sick. And you have this idea Warren is going to lend you some money—"

"Edna called Bergie," Timothy J. Heaney says, "Your worries where I was were over then. But Warren turned me down. He claims he put all the money he had into the Nash dealership. I don't think it's much of a dealership, tell you the truth—"

"Nash ain't much of a car," Hack Devlin says, "Starters ain't worth a damn—"

"Tim," Nell Kemp, a legal secretary, worked for a lawyer anyway before she married Wesley L. Kemp, putting her oar in, says, "You must been bonded, Tim, administer The Estate? Were you, are you, bonded?"

"Yes," Timothy J. Heaney, sighing like he's just about run out of air and doubts he'll find any more, says. "Fifteen-thousand-dollar surety bond. Same with those insurance companies. I was bonded, I was their agent. You all have recourse, The Estate. File a complaint, bond company will make good on The Estate. Then come after me, I guess. Charge me with malfeasance or something, I can't come up with fifteen-thousand. Put me in jail then, maybe—"

Old Tim's Estate

"Nobody's going to jail!" Bergda, though she doesn't sound absolutely certain about this, says, and another heavy silence descends.

In the kitchen, Edith, smoothing white frosting on the angel food cake, asks Eddie, "What are they talking about?"

"Putting your dad in jail," Eddie reports.

"Oh, no!" Edith wails and starts crying, dribbling tears on the frosting. "Come over here! You shouldn't be listening to them!" But Eddie goes right on listening.

"Well of course we don't want Tim to go to jail," Ceil, who doesn't sound absolutely certain about this either, says. "But what I think, I think we should all have a talk. Under the circumstances. All the rest of us, I mean. You, Nell, and Gert, and our husbands, and Bee and Henry and Emma. This is a serious family matter. The Estate and all. I think we should sit down and discuss it. Right this minute since we're all here together. I know Edith's getting cake and coffee ready. But I think we should go someplace else and discuss it. In private."

There's general assent, none of it reluctant, the West College Street Heaneys voice no protest and the other Heaneys and the three husbands and Emma and Young Charlie Goggins pull on their coats. Eddie's called from the kitchen, deprived of any cake, Edith still sniffling, and puts on his jacket.

"We'll phone you, we've come to some decisions," Ceil tells the Timothy J. Heaneys and the clan and their spouses and Young Charlie and Eddie depart, no warm words exchanged.

They drive in their three cars, Henry Heaney's is a spavined '24 Plymouth four-door, to the Princess Cafe on Broadway, open until eleven p.m. Saturdays but half empty, gather at a rear table, order pie and coffee, milk for Eddie, the Princess famous for its "home-baked pies," and Ceil opens the proceedings.

"I knew Tim was fooling around with The Estate," Ceil says, "the minute we found out he was in the Stock Market! But I didn't say anything. I guess I didn't want to worry anybody. Or maybe I was hoping he wasn't. Fooling around with The Estate, I mean. I was hoping our brother was honest. I thought he knew better than to fool around with insurance companies' money too. And I certainly didn't ever think he'd mortgage our house! Right out from under us! What do you all think we should do?"

Nobody seems to know (or wants to say) apparently and the discussion, spiced with many unkind remarks regarding Timothy J. Heaney nobody had the nerve to voice in his house, drags on. Eddie listens to some of this but soon grows bored. He takes a look at the Princess' menu (Pie 10 Cents, Chicken Chow Mien With Dinner Roll 35 Cents, Choice of Roast Goose Ham or Yankee Pot Roast With Stuffing and Vegetable 50 Cents) then studies the big mural on the rear wall. It depicts some ancient battle scene, knights in armor on horses sticking lances in each other, Sir Edward the Fearless born seven-hundred years too late.

The unfortunate fact is Henry and Emma Heaney, Nell and Wesley L. Kemp and Gert and Old Charlie Goggins (except for his hernia) had no immediate overriding financial interest in The Estate and nothing at all to do with the house in Stiles. Henry got the farm and title to same and Nell and Gert got $2500 each and that was that, and Old Charlie says he can put his hernia operation off for awhile. Old Charlie's a large peaceable man with a crumpled face who detests family squabbles: he had enough of those growing up, then Young Charlie, in another Irish household wracked by drink. Nell and Wesley L. Kemp are healthy, have no kids, Wesley made a few dollars in the Stock Market, and the little ulcer he had is all cleared up. Wesley's a hog buyer for the B&P Meat Packing Co., a pretty good job: he and Nell have money in the bank.

But all this, in Ceil's view, has nothing to do with the Devlins' situation and Bee's. "Where are we," she says, again, "ever going to get twenty dollars a month for a mortgage payment? For a house supposed to be ours till we die!"

Hack Devlin opens his mouth then closes it. Twenty dollars a month for a mortgage payment right off the top of his meager income for twenty years, Ceil no doubt moaning about it the whole time,

Old Tim's Estate

dampens his usual optimism. Besides, this really is something the Heaneys have to wrestle with: it was their Estate.

"And what about the money for college?" Ceil says, "That's all gone too! Tim took it!" But there's not much response to this indictment: there are no teetotaling young Heaneys of good character college bound—not yet anyway. Ceil tries again. "Besides, my god, there's the principle of the thing! It was our money if we ever needed it and Tim took it! Nell, you know about these thing. Exactly what would happen if we, what is it, file a complaint with that bond company Tim mentioned?"

"Well," Nell, drawing on her legal experience, says, "the bond company would make good on the Estate all right. Then come after Tim for that money. Take him to court probably. If Tim didn't have the money and that's the way it sounds, the bond company probably go after his house. Any equity he has in it. But he said he took a second mortgage on their house. Not much equity left, probably. Bond company might file some charge then. Malfeasance. Misappropriation of Funds. Failure to Maintain Fiduciary Trust. Something like that. That'd be a criminal charge. Tim might wind up in jail, I guess. Or prison. For awhile. Not very long, I don't think. Year or two maybe. That's the hard cheese—"

"Oh, I don't want Tim to go to jail!" Bee says, or wails. "Or gosh, prison! Our own brother! That would kill Dad! If he was alive. Mother too. And like Bergda said, Tim didn't know the Stock Market was going to, well, what it did. CRASH or Black Thursday, whatever—"

"He knew how to get his hands on The Estate, though," Ceil says, "and our house! I guess we can be thankful Dad and Mother aren't alive, see this mess. But what in the world are we going to do about it? Are we just going to let Tim get away with it? Go on his merry way?"

There's a lengthy silence while the other clan members, presumably, weigh the relative merits of resurrecting The Estate against the awful disgrace they'll all have to live with if in fact Timothy J. Heaney, their very own brother, is packed off to jail—or prison.

"My suggestion," Wesley L. Kemp says, "is take a vote on it." He'd

T.R. St. George

like to get home, since nobody wants to hear about his coup in the Stock Market, play some golf Sunday at Fairbow's Municipal Links, then take it easy because Monday's a big day, a dozen farmers with fat hogs to sell to see and haggle with, jew down. "Vote you're gonna file a complaint with that bond company or not."

"Secret ballot," Old Charlie Goggins the peacemaker says, "Just the Heaneys. It's their Estate. Was, I mean. We can use napkins. You wanna file a complaint, vote Yes. You don't, vote No."

"Young Charlie should vote too," Gert Goggins says, "It was him found Tim's car and him and Yegga expecting another baby and all—"

"Well, all right," Ceil says, "but if Young Charlie votes, Edward should too." But Edward, Nell says, isn't old enough to vote. Nevertheless, Ceil says, Edward is present and has just as much stake in The Estate as Young Charlie. Young Charlie, a peacable man at heart like his father, solves this impasse. He doesn't want to vote, he says, it don't seem to him like The Estate's any his business. Eddie, beginning to confront a dilemma, which way to vote, relaxes and resumes his study of the knights in armor sticking lances in each other.

"Okay," Old Charlie, handing our napkins says, "Just the five Heaneys then—"

"No, I ain't voting," Henry Heaney says, "I got the farm and I ain't sick. Em neither or the kids. I ain't involve in this and I don't wanna be."

But Henry's siblings say he has to vote, he or Em or their kids might be sick someday and it's a family matter, he can't duck it. Henry caves in and they vote, using Wesley Kemp's fake gold fountain pen, and Old Charlie counts the ballots. Two Yes, two No, one Abstain.

"Damn you, Henry!" Ceil, swearing again in Eddie's presence, says. "You always were stubborn! We'll vote again and you vote, one way or the other?"

"Awright!" Henry says, "I'm gonna vote No then! You always tryin' push me around, Ceil. Long as I remember."

"Two Yes then, three No," Old Charlie the election judge says,

Old Tim's Estate

and there the matter rests—or dies. Timothy J. Heaney won't go to jail or prison or his siblings at any rate won't take any action likely to put him behind bars.

On their way home, chugging along in the Model T,. Eddie half asleep in the rear seat with Bee, Bee confesses she voted No.

"I knew that," Ceil says, "You and Nell, I suppose. She doesn't need the money. I'm sure Gert voted Yes, Charlie's hernia. Damn that Henry! And Wesley Kemp! We should have talked about it more before we voted. That was Wesley's idea, vote right away, sticking his nose in our business, a family matter. Him and the money he made in the Stock Market! Nell told me all about that, we were talking on the phone Thursday. Wesley took three-hundred dollars out of their saving account the middle of August, didn't tell Nell, and bought some stocks. That Blue Ridge or something. But then he started worrying he might lose his three-hundred dollars and couldn't sleep. Tossed and turned for a week. Nell finally asked him what was wrong and he told her and Nell made him sell the stocks and get out of the damn Stock Market. He made about sixty dollars and now he thinks he's J.P. Morgan! I just hope, Bee, you're all satisfied now! You and Nell and Henry. We'll always be poor now! Poorer than we are. I feel sorry for Bergda and the girls. Or maybe they knew all along, the whole time, what our dear brother Tim was up to. That wouldn't surprise me. Them and their fancy house and that big radio. All their new cars. I think Tim deserves a little time in jail! Do him good!"

"Oh no!" Bee says, "I think Tim's got trouble enough. And he said he'll help us out with the house, he gets back on his feet—"

"That'll be the day!" Ceil says, "Tim's broke. He ever gets back on his feet you can bet he'll buy another big damn radio before he helps us!"

"You should phone them though," Bee says, "soon's when we get home. Tell them, you know, we voted and all—"

"No, not tonight," Ceil says, "I'll call them tomorrow. Collect. It's late and it'll do them good, wonder and worry awhile. Like I am. Oh god, Bee! What are going to do about our house? We can't make mortgage payments, twenty dollars a month. Where will we live if the bank takes our house!"

That's a thought so frightening, The Bank taking their house, it keeps Eddie, curled up in his cot thirty minutes later, wide awake for an hour, tossing and turning like Wesley L. Kemp when he was in the Stock Market, while downstairs Ceil and Hack and Bee discuss the grim situation they now confront—a mumble of voices when Ceil's not sniffling. There was a picture in The Weekly Reader, a whole bunch of Mexicans who pick lettuce or something in California and don't have a house so they live in their car, a beat-up old Reo it looked like. But there's no way there'd be room in the Model T for him and Ceil and Hack and Bee and their clothes and where would they eat and where would Bee cook?

Asleep finally, Eddie dreams his Uncle Tim is in prison, a prisoner, wearing those clothes that look like pajamas with black-and-white stripes and chains on his legs so he can't escape like the prisoners on the Georgia Chain Gang there was a picture of in The Weekly Reader. This dream gives way to one far worse in which the First National Bank comes and takes their house, jacking it up and hauling it away on big rollers with a truck, the way Al Morris and his dad jacked up an old boxcar without wheels abandoned by the MSP&P near the water tank and hauled it with Al's truck to behind Claude Clarke's store, so Claude could add an ice-house to his empire.

7.

This disaster, however, does not immediately come to pass. Timothy J. Heaney, good as his word, goes and talks to the First National Bank of Winatchee Falls and the First National Bank, though somewhat reluctant, lets the Devlins assume the three-thousand dollar mortgage. They also get title to the property, subject to the mortgage, which Ceil at any rate thinks a step in the right direction.

Two long miserable years then pass, by which time Eddie—never having seen another birthday dollar from his Uncle Tim—is twelve and in the sixth grade in the Big Room. The Devlins and Bee, Ceil keeping a close watch on their pennies, struggle throughout these years to come up with $28.85 a month for the First National Bank (Timothy J. Heaney forgot or at any rate omitted to include the property taxes and insurance in his $20-a-month estimate) but Ceil, often beset by miserable headaches, was right: they frequently are unable to make that payment.

The Great Depression sets in, for one thing. Hack's garage business, never robust, slows, and Bee's ten percent of Henry Heaney's cash crop income, corn down to 18 cents bushel, proves insignificant. They're six months behind with the mortgage payments when the First National Bank in a registered letter thoughtfully mailed the week before Christmas, noting it's been "extremely patient," forecloses on the mortgage, though granting the mortgagees "as provided by law" six months in which to make all the payments "by then due" and "redeem or renegotiate the said mortgage."

Everybody in Stiles soon knows this: Claude Clarke the Postmaster knows what registered letters from banks usually portend and blabs. Several residents in similar circumstances subsequently commiserate with Ceil and Hack and Bee, but a lot of good that does, and Ceil makes a command decision. Since "there's no way on God's green earth" they can make twelve mortgage payments in six months, they won't even try. They'll keep up the insurance (it covers storm damage, fire insurance no longer offered Stiles homeowners in view of the long history of conflagrations in the village) but let the taxes slide and "won't send the damn bank another damn cent," swearing again in Eddie's presence but this is another crisis.

Which they don't. The six months pass. Swiftly, it seems. The First National Bank sends another registered letter, this one stating that "as provided by law, the holder of said mortgage, to wit, The First National Bank of Winatchee Falls, will take possession of the aforesaid hereinafter described real property within ten (10) days"—come and take their house!—and the Devlins and Bee perforce must move from ("vacate on or before July 10") the aforesaid house: their house but not any more.

The Devlins move to Winatchee Falls the Monday after the 1932 Fourth of July Picnic at Precious Blood, because Hack gets a job there fixing cars at Cheesy Adams' Day & Night Garage, very lucky to get this job what with The Great Depression growing more depressing by the day. They borrow Poop Clarke's truck. Several neighbors supervised by Ernie Hoff pitch in and help Hack load the truck and Marlin Poole goes with Hack to help unload the furniture they take with them. Their clothes, dishes, pots and pans and so on, Ceil's books and sundry memorabilia are packed in the Model T, Eddie's bike lashed on top. Herb Bender's drafted to drive the Model T and drive Poop's truck back to Stiles. Ernie Hoff's moving too: he'll be rooming-and-boarding at the Boettcher's, much to Miss Mott's dismay, and

Old Tim's Estate

Frank Pratt will be eating at the Gibbons now, much to his dismay: Luverne's cooking is not highly rated and her servings are skimpy by Frank's standards.

Eddie, though boys twelve-going-on-thirteen are not supposed to cry, comes pretty close to crying while watching this evacuation—leaving the only house he ever lived in, the house in fact in which he was delivered by old Mrs. Kelly before she got the dropsy—but doesn't, not with all the kids in town present. He perks up some when Buddy Douglas, Hinty Murphy, Bunkie Olson and Margie Bremer all say they wish they were moving to Winatchee Falls—where they guess Eddie "prolly gonna see a movie ever day." Eddie also, this a kind of official farewell, lights off some left-over firecrackers with Buddy, blowing empty tin cans high in the air. And Margie Bremer, embarrassing him, gives him a little hug, squashing her chest, which is growing, against his.

Ceil doesn't cry either, though Bee does, a little. Eddie was pretty sure Ceil would but Old Tim Heaney's pioneer genes apparently kick in when this move becomes inevitable. Ceil in fact pretty much organizes it and finds them a place to live, a one-bedroom upstairs apartment, $18 a month, one month in advance, in an old remodeled house called a four-plex on Eleventh Avenue on Winatchee Falls' far East Side six blocks shy of Sheeny's Junkyard. Actually, Estelle Heaney finds this apartment. Ceil seeks Estelle's help, figuring Estelle can't very well in the circumstances prevailing refuse, and subsequently thanks Estelle, though briefly. Ceil also organizes a Yard Sale outside their house in Stiles and sells some of their furniture secondhand, furniture Bee doesn't want that won't fit in the one-bedroom apartment. This sale produces $64, which Ceil sticks in her purse along with the $84 left from the money they saved while making no mortgage payments to the First National Bank. That's earmarked in part for some fillings in his teeth Eddie needs. Bee takes some of the furniture, the old rooster and most of the Rhode Island Reds, shooing them into a big crate, a sort of portable chicken coop Herb built for her with scrap lumber and chickenwire, which

151

Poop will haul to the Bender farm after the move to Winatchee Falls. Four hens escape, join the Hock flock and the Hocks promptly eat them.

Bee takes most of the Rhode Island Reds.

Bee's getting ready to marry Herb Bender two weeks hence, it'll be a quiet wedding in the Precious Blood church, and will stay with the Henry Heaneys meanwhile. Old Mrs. Bender went to her eternal reward, finally, the middle of May. Some Good Christians think Herb and Bee should wait awhile, six months anyway, show the old lady some respect, but Herb, his independent streak bubbling up, said, "The hell with that, we wait about ten years awready."

The house in Stiles—the First National Bank, sure enough, comes and "takes" it though leaving it where it was—stands empty for nearly a year, then Milo Stacowitz the Section Gang foreman sells two lots in Winona nobody knew he had and buys it, paying the back taxes.

"At a very good price, we understand," Ceil often says, "I guess the Bank just wanted to get rid of it." She sometimes adds, bitterly, "Your

Old Tim's Estate

grandfather's house, Eddie! Our house! But those Polacks are living in it now!"

Eddie, going on fourteen, sometimes wonders: is Lorrie Stacowitz sleeping in his old room? And sometimes thinks, though this no doubt is a deadly Unclean Thought, it might be sort of fun to crawl into his cot there with Lorrie and sort of, well, snuggle up to her. This and similar deadly Unclean Thoughts he makes no determined effort to put from his mind often assail Eddie now when, home alone with Ceil, he goes to bed on the pull-out couch in the living room in their one-bedroom apartment. They're home alone nights because Hack's the night man at Cheesy Adams' Day & Night Garage, six p.m. to six a.m. every night except Sunday, paid $18 a week.

Uncle Dick Devlin fixed that. Dick's still on Cheesy's payroll on straight commissions, no draw, selling an occasional Plymouth, the low end of the line, or a used car, though car sales have taken a deep dive since The Great Depression began. "Hack's a hell of a mechanic," Dick told Cheesy when the former night man, Karl Klechner, he was seventy-two, got the arthritis and had to pack it in and this far more important in Cheesy's view, "Hack'll work cheap."

"Too cheap," Ceil often says, "but at least there's a little money coming in," this a reference to the fact Hack's garage business in Stiles eventually just collapsed. Everybody still owes him. Ceil, taking the helm with Old Tim Heaney's genes, writes these deadbeats at intervals, phones them even, those who have phones, late in the evening when the long-distance rates go down , demanding payment, and now and then a deadbeat sends a check for $3 or $5. But they mostly all have terrible tales of woe, claim they're flat broke, blame The Great Depression.

The Great Depression's omnipresent, a grim fact of life, the National Unemployment Rate at 25 percent, bankers no longer pronouncing The Market "sound." In Stiles (Ceil get reports from the deadbeats) Gail Poole's moved in with Frank Pratt, replacing the mysterious ex-lady friend, creating a minor scandal, and is cooking

TR. St. George

for Frank, who soon grew tired of Luverne Gibbons' skimpy cuisine and replaced his pot-bellied stove with a bottle-gas stove. They eat a lot of day-old bakery products the Tastee Bread truck delivers and Frank's cut the price of a game of pool, formerly ten cents, to a nickel, the third game free, but few Stiles pool players have that kind of money. A summer thunderstorm, winds clocked at 70 mph, blew the Frank's Billiards & Refreshments sign off the poolhall, but Frank's not replaced it, can't afford that. Frank thought Happy Days Were Here Again when Congress scuttled Prohibition and he got a 3.2 beer license, beer in metal barrels the Hamn's Brewery truck delivers and a tap with which to dispense it. But few customers have money for beer, much of it foam, at a nickel a glass. Banty Shanahan still gets his Veteran's Pension but he's digging adult graves for a dollar and been known to nurse a nickel beer for two hours between Pension checks. Most of the Stiles Hotel old-timers who depend on farm income are way behind in their rent what with crop prices at an all-time low, but Lee J. Lilly's not got the heart to evict them, no other place they can go, the County Poor Farm filled to capacity and more. Claude Clarke no longer sells groceries on credit or gets any from S. Dolan & Sons without cash on the barrel head. Poop Clarke's Ford truck is falling apart, but milk and cream are hardly worth hauling anyway, the prices the Co-op Dairy is paying. Ernie Hoff and Miss Mott are keeping the Boettchers going. Joe Boettcher's virtually unemployed though called in by the chicken hatchery for a day or so now and then to candle eggs or something. The Boettcher kids, Ben and Jerry, are sleeping in a bunk-bed in their parents' bedroom, sex there as elsewhere pretty much on hold, the nation's birthrate sinking fast while The Great Depression rages. Joe's not up to that anyway while the $400 he had in a Savings Account slowly dwindles.

Ernie's rolling his own cigarettes with a little machine he bought and worried sick, boring everybody at the poolhall with his tale of woe: there's a rumor the Frohoeft Lumber Co. might close the Stiles

Old Tim's Estate

lumberyard. Ernie hosed down his sheepskin coat and still has his leather helmet and goggles but evinces no further interest whatsoever in aviation, stormbarning going, loop-the-loops looping or rides at County Fairs giving. He paid Hack Devlin and Al Morris $10 each on account for their labor on his airplane but no more. The banged up airplane lies abandoned behind Al's Repair Shop, most of its fabric gone, weeds growing through it. Al, busy fixing broken farm machinery since nobody can afford new machinery in the middle of The Great Depression, never did get around to rebuilding the airplane. He did salvage the engine though, gave Hack Devlin $10 for it and installed it on the snowmobile he's building: a Model T chassis set on runners powered by a big propeller the engine will spin, which he saw pictured in Popular Mechanics Magazine. Al's theory as to the crash that abruptly terminated the airplane's first and only flight—he inspected the control cables when removing the engine—is Ernie, confused, did a dumb thing: he pushed the joystick forward instead of pulling it back when the airplane lifted off, thus producing an immediate terminal nose-dive. Ernie, still a stubborn German, won't discuss this theory.

The MSP&P, bankrupt again though many nonpaying passengers are riding its freights, dropped its eight a.m. and three p.m. passenger service to Stiles a year ago. The Omaha Flyer still rolls through but carries few paying passengers and the boxcars parked on the long Stiles spur often remain there for weeks, empty. The Section Gang's been reduced to Milo Stacowitz and Franz Geist, working three days a week. Barney Poole and Marlin hit the road to look for work when that happened, hopping a westbound freight, and have not been heard from since. Old Mrs. Poole went to the County Poor Farm then, the last indigent admitted, and Gail moved in with Frank Pratt: they're trying to sell the old lady's house but can't find a buyer. Werner Bremer, unemployed, turned to bootlegging, proved inept, was apprehended as Prohibition wound down and is halfway through a year-and-a-day in the Leavenworth Federal Prison. Some think Frank Pratt snitched on

T.R. St. George

Werner. The Bremers are six months behind with their rent, $15 a month for the old house Harry Kelly owns, and Harry (like a cruel British landlord) is threatening to evict them. The Bremers are trying to get on The Welfare—a revolutionary new concept engineered by President Franklin D. Roosevelt and the Democrats and roundly condemned by the Republicans, who consider government help for the shiftless poor the nation's first step on the Road to Perdition—but haven't managed that because Werner, technically, is not available for work. Margie Bremer and her sister Sylvia, lugging the four-year-old boy they call Bert, are out every day in the summer picking dandelion greens and swiping produce from other people's garden for the Bremer's skimpy larder. Kerm Bremer lied about his age and joined the CCCs (Civilian Conservation Corps). He's cutting brush or building trails or something in the Superior National Forest, buying cigarettes cheap and sending $10 a month home. And Sylvia's pregnant again, "six months gone" the report is, Bert Murphy again thought to be the nigger in the woodpile.

Herb Bender's still farming, scratching out a living, No. 2 Yellow Corn fetching but 15 cents a bushel. Herb and Bee frequently visit the Devlins in Winatchee Falls and Bee always brings something to eat, a pie or cake or a hot dish, fresh vegetables in season, tomatoes or something she canned. Ceil's cooking for Hack and Eddie, though somewhat "leery" of the gas stove in their apartment and that's not her favorite occupation anyway. But Ceil's holding up pretty well, all things considered, Old Tim Heaney's pioneer genes still at work. She's still watching their pennies, of course, and wishes they had a larger apartment with a bedroom for Eddie, but likes living in Winatchee Falls. There are a lot more things to do in Winatchee Falls than in Stiles. She's joined The Friends of the Public Library and been appointed to the Membership Committee. Hack Devlin's happy enough fixing cars, the repair business booming since few can afford a new car in the middle of The Great Depression.

Old Tim's Estate

The 1930 Census counted 21,005 permanent residents in Winatchee Falls (including 312 in the State Hospital for the Insane on the city's far north side) and, 20,971 in Fairbow—a signal victory for Winatchee Falls.

Eddie also like life in the city. The first summer was sort of tough. He was the new kid on the block and at the Hawthorne School Playground, a target for the normal savagery, and had a few fights, losing some, some undeclared draws. Russell Schneider, the neighborhood bully, a big kid, seventeen years old, beat him up pretty good, bloodied his nose and raised a big welt on his cheek. Ceil, much to Eddie's amazement, did not throw a fit when he stumbled home bloody and bowed after this fight with Russ, like she always did in Stiles. She just said he might as well get used to it, people like Russ Schneider—life was hard and likely to remain so.

But that's all ancient history now. Two more new kids moved into the neighborhood, so Eddie's no longer the new kid and Russ Schneider's no longer a menace. Caught red-handed stealing hubcaps from Sheeny's Junkyard, Russ is in the Red Wing Reform School learning auto mechanics and eight ways to hot-wire other people's cars.

Eddie walks or rides his bike halfway across Winatchee Falls to school and back, the seventh grade at Holy Redeemer, often lingering on his way home on Broadway, the current center of his universe, with Chester (Chesty) Bennett, a classmate and his new best friend—a chunky blond kid who used to be a Holy Redeemer altar boy but was fired for sampling the sacramental wine. Chesty's two months older than Eddie and, growing up in the city, far wiser. Chesty's pretty worldly. They sometimes ease into Hub Horlick's Cigar Store after school to look at the pictures of practically naked girls, Chesty's an expert in this field, in some of the magazines there, Captain Billy's Whiz Bang and The Police Gazette, until Hub orders them out.

T.R. St. George

Life in the city.

Some church ladies scandalized by reports regarding those and similar magazines once talked Winatchee Falls City Attorney D.J. Mahoney into charging Hub with contributing to the delinquency of minors. Nothing came of that. Hub's lawyer, August Schott, Chesty knows the whole story, "revoked Hub's First Amendment Rights and old Judge Gutknecht throwed it out the Court." But Hub doesn't want any more trouble with the church ladies.

Sometimes, Clyde Dobermann, old Dollar Dobermann's son, heir to the Dobermann Hotel and other holdings, if he's buying cigarettes at Hub's, joins them at the magazine rack. Clyde's the richest kid in town—or was, he's not a kid anymore, he's twenty-one and was going to college somewhere but dropped out. He's big, six feet tall, weighs two-hundred pounds, which is sort of funny because old Dollar Dobermann's a tiny little man. No bigger than a peanut hardly. Clyde has some kind of job at the hotel but doesn't spend much time there. He plays golf a lot in the summer and has is own car, a red Pontiac

Old Tim's Estate

convertible he drives like he was in the Indianapolis 500. In fact, Clyde's been arrested once already for drunk driving. But on account of his dad's old Dollar Dobermann, Chesty knows the whole story, he finally was charged instead with careless driving and fined $10. Chesty would like to be Clyde, or just like Clyde, when he grows up and always strikes up a conversation with Clyde at the magazine rack. Like they were old friends. But Clyde, Eddie surmises, doesn't have any idea who Chesty is.

Eddie would like to go to the public high school, Winatchee Falls High, when he gets out of the eighth grade. At Holy Redeemer High he'd have to take Latin and probably be an altar boy. Ceil would like that but Chesty's warned Eddie. The new altar boys always get the six o'clock Mass in the winter, have to get up at five a.m., it's still dark, the middle of the night, the temperature twenty below zero, and slog through the snowdrifts to the Holy Redeemer church, which is "colder'n a witch's tit." Chesty will be going to the public high. His mother, her name's Pauline, she's divorced or thinks she is and a physical therapist at the Pretzell Chiropractic Clinic, can't afford the $20 a semester tuition at Holy Redeemer High. Lorrie Stacowitz, once Stile's best student, skipped another grade (this a report from a deadbeat) and already goes to Winatchee Falls High. She's a freshman and stays with one of her aunts on school nights. Eddie's seen Lorrie once or twice downtown but not to talk to.

Ceil's not sure she "really approves" of Chesty. He's always very polite, removes his cap if he's wearing one, calls Ceil "Missus Devlin." But his mother's divorced—well, not really, she's Catholic or was, supposed to be, can't be divorced, but seems to think she is—and has boy friends. Ceil's not yet said Eddie can go to the public high but she's thinking about it, the $20 a semester tuition the main thing she's thinking about.

Henry Heaney's still farming, there isn't anything else he knows how to do, and beginning to wish he'd voted Yes that night at the Princess Cafe, sent his own brother to jail maybe but resurrected The

T. R. St. George

Estate. Henry's pretty close to some dire need. Corn's scarcely worth picking and it costs more to raise pigs and cows, feed them and ship them than they fetch at the B&P Meat Packing Co. Henry had to go to the Hayfield State Bank & Trust and mortgage one of his eighties, it's not free and clear anymore, to buy seed and keep on farming. That would kill Old Tim Heaney, he who hated bankers, if he were alive. And Little Tim Heaney, old Doc Dempsey says, should have his tonsils and adenoids out and it looks like Emma might need a gallbladder operation—but she's putting that off for awhile.

Timothy J. Heaney almost goes to jail anyway. The bonding companies, there were two, that provided the bonds he had to have when an agent for Mutual of Omaha, The Prudential and so on—after settling up with the insurance companies for the $2600 in premiums Tim used to boost his margins and lost in the CRASH—come after Tim like hungry tigers on the prowl. One calls what Tim did Failure to Maintain Fiduciary Trust and Misappropriation of Funds. The other one calls it Grand Theft and it's nip and tuck for awhile, but Tim manages to squeak out of this bind. He sells his fancy house on West College Street, taking a big loss, but gets $1200 in equity he had in it out of it. He sells his new Buick, taking another big loss, but gets $300 out of it. Bergda sells her crystal collection, her fur coat, her jewelry and the big Silver Echo radio. Peggy Connell—an office girl at the Adolph Mensch Insurance Agency, still suspect though swearing on her Rosary and her mother's grave it wasn't her blabbed about Tim to the Bugle Call—buys the Silver Echo. Estelle takes half her life's savings, $600, out of the First National Bank—Timothy J. Heaney, resigned, no longer a director there—and the late Old Sam Dolan's sons reluctantly, just to keep her father out of jail, advance her $300 against her salary, that cut to $17 a week in view of The Great Depression. These various sums satisfy the bonding companies and they back off, withdrawing their complaints.

Tim also, it develops, owes the First National Bank $1500 on a personal note gone with the CRASH. But that's a civil matter and the First National Bank eventually just writes it off—a bad debt. It's not

Old Tim's Estate

the only one. Arnold Felke, a failure at suicide and the former First National president, also resigned, discharged from the Community Hospital, sporting a hairpiece, is found to have misappropriated, embezzled, around $18,000 in bank funds—all gone with the CRASH. Arnold promptly sells his house on West College Street, subject to a lien the bank slaps on it, and departs in the night for California, a popular Midwestern solution to just about any problem. Despite some halfhearted efforts, he's not been brought to justice. The First National is thought to be "pretty shaky" for awhile but survives, subsequently (as earlier noted) foreclosing on numerous farm and home mortgages.

The Timothy J. Heaneys also survive. They move from West College Street into a little East Side house they rent on Tenth Avenue, four blocks from the Devlins' apartment. Tim finds this house after the First National Bank forecloses on it and, since hardly anybody is buying houses in the middle of The Great Depression, puts it on the rental market. Tim still has friends at the bank. Edith does not go to St. Benedict's and take Home Ec but on graduating with good marks from Holy Redeemer High, third in her class, gets a part-time job in Accounts Receivable at The Chiro. Bergda also goes to work, three days a week in Ladies Foundations at Knowlton's Department Store, twenty-two cents an hour, lucky to get that position. Timothy J. Heaney gives up his social membership at the Golf & Country Club (he's not the only one), drops out of the Lions Club, the Kiwanis and the Knights of Columbus and begins to "look around" for work, meanwhile mowing the yard, raking the leaves and shoveling the sidewalk at the rented house in season and helping some with the housework. He also abandons his weekly visit to Nick Swanger's barbershop, Bergda trims his fringe of gray hair, but still wears a three-piece suit and spats at all times, even when mowing the yard or shoveling the sidewalk, and the gold watch chain on his vest, though this chain no longer leads to Old Tim Heaney's gold watch. The gold watch is in Leon Shapira's Pawn Shop, the $15 Leon "allowed" on it spent on a Christmas present for Bergda, a crystal candy dish, in 1932.

T.R. St. George

Timothy J. Heaney "looks around" for two years then, likewise lucky in the middle of The Great Depression, goes back to work, becoming the night auditor at the Dobermann Hotel, by far the best and biggest of Winatchee Falls' six hotels, this count including the Moon Beam Motel out on Highway 61. Old Hein (Dollar) Dobermann, a self-made man and Winatchee Falls' leading financier—otherwise busy buying farms and other real estate foreclosed on by various banks until Roosevelt and the Democrats, confounding and enraging old Dobermann and many bankers, impose a temporary moratorium on farm foreclosures—does not bond Timothy J. Heaney or even try to. But Tim was always good with figures and his previous financial difficulties by this time are ancient history, pretty much forgotten. Tim's not the only former leading Winatchee Falls businessman adapting to a new life style following the Stock Market CRASH and what with The Great Depression still going strong, no end to it in sight, just about everybody except Dollar Dobermann and the Pretzell Brothers (bad backs and The Chiro pretty much Depression-proof) seems to be facing financial difficulties.

Timothy J. Heaney promptly gets Old Tim's gold watch out of hock, Leon Shapira (a pretty good fellow for a Jew, everybody says) having granted many extensions on the usual ninety-day redemption period. Tim also buys a used '27 Buick, pays a sign-painter to paint T.J.H. in old English script under the front-door handles, resumes his weekly haircuts and revives his memberships in the Lions, the Kiwanis and the KCs and the KCs presently elect him Treasurer. Estelle, still the bookkeeper at S. Dolan & Sons—she'll be there forever, that $300 advance she's slowly repaying guarantees her lifetime employment—subsequently withdraws the rest of her life's savings, saved by the Bank Holiday declared by Roosevelt, and makes a down payment on the rented house with a contract-for-deed at $30 a month, title to same in her name fifteen years hence.

"Estelle's no fool," Ceil says, when told this by Hack, who hears it from a guy who brings his Nash into the day & Night Garage for a new

Old Tim's Estate

starter whose brother is married to a woman whose sister has a friend in the Mortgage Department at the First National Bank.

The Devlins throughout these years, though living in the same neighborhood, do not see much of the Timothy J. Heaneys. Neither do the other Heaney siblings. The other Heaney siblings, like the Devlins, are not exactly "not speaking" to the Timothy J. Heaneys, but they aren't exactly speaking to them either. The Estate's gone but not forgotten and the Timothy J. Heaneys, no doubt wisely, no longer come to the Fourth of July Picnics at Precious Blood. Edith and Estelle, even Bergda, make an effort, heal this rift. They send though they do not for a year or so receive Christmas cards and birthday cards, remember Eddie's birthday and send him presents, clothes usually, much to his disgust: Bergda gets a discount at Knowlton's. And now and then, if Eddie runs into his Uncle Tim the night auditor somewhere downtown, Uncle Tim slips him a dime—The Great Depression equivalent of a quarter.

Eddie's pretty clear now as to what the terrible thing Timothy J. Heaney did was: he took all the money was in Old Tim Heaney's Estate and lost it when the Stock Market CRASHED and got some money for the house in Stiles from the First National Bank and lost that money too and the house in the CRASH. A terrible thing or two terrible things. But on the other hand, Eddie often thinks, it was Uncle Tim's shenanigans more or less propelled the Devlins to Winatchee Falls. But for Uncle Tim and his shenanigans they'd most likely still be living in Stiles. A one-horse burg if ever there was one. So, whatever it was Uncle Tim did, it really was what they call a blessing in a disguise. Eddie bears him no ill will.

With one of Tim's dimes and a nickel Eddie can go to a movie—a double-feature, a comedy, a serial and a newsreel—at the Empress Theater on Broadway. Or sometimes he and Chesty Bennett buy one ticket and draw lots to see who goes into the Empress and opens the fire door into the alley about six inches so whoever lost the draw can sneak in. The trick is to wait for a really exciting sequence on the

T.R. St. George

screen, everybody watching the good guys and the bad guys galloping through the sagebrush or the fierce Indians attacking the wagon-train or the prelude to the climatic gunfight, and get in fast before an usher sees the daylight leaking in the fire door. They've been caught a couple of times, summarily ejected by the head usher, Brewster Hendershott, and Banned For Life from the Empress, which means a week, but more often than not they get away with this little scam and spend the fifteen cents they save on pop or candy or something at Hub Horlick's cigar store. Buddy Douglas will turn deep green with envy, he ever hears about life in the city. Chesty and Eddie are both Boy Scouts, Tenderfeet without uniforms, they can't afford uniforms, in Troop 27 at Holy Redeemer, but feel some of the Twelve Scout Laws—Honest, Trustworthy and so on—do not necessarily apply in the middle of The Great Depression.

Eddie has other friends—Phil Karn, Stub Olson, Dingy Young (his folks own the Moon Beam Motel), Johnnie Keefe, Henry Miller, Lew Watoski, Junior Sheeny (heir to the Junkyard), Lennie Hines, Billy Mitchell—but Chesty's his best friend. All these friends are East Siders and—except for Chesty, Eddie and and Billy Mitchell—they go to Hawthorne School. They're kind of a gang but loosely organized. They have no colors, initiation rites or meetings. Chesty's sort of the leader. Their base is the Hawthorne School Playground. They spend hours there, shooting baskets or playing pickup softball or football or shinny in the winter when the playground's turned into a skating rink, and talking about stuff, mainly sports and girls. Sex. Eddie's learned a lot about girls and sex, much of it erroneous, but has no real handle yet on Life: his Life or Life in General. Sometimes on hot summer days they drift from the playground and go swimming in the Winatchee River where it winds through the Municipal Golf Course, upstream from where it's posted No Swimming on account of the stuff the Co-op Dairy dumps in it. They dive there for golf balls duffers playing the fourth and fifteenth holes hit into the river, which the pro at the Muny, Bobbie Santrapp, will buy for a nickel each if

Old Tim's Estate

they're not cut. The planned Municipal Swimming Pool remains a blueprint, the bonds issued to finance its construction failing to find any buyers once The Great Depression set in.

These salvaged golf balls and rare odd-jobs mowing somebody's grass or raking leaves on West College Street are just about their only sources of income. Junior Sheeny gets an allowance, thought to be $1 a week, but won't share it: Junior's no philanthropist. Chesty had a job for awhile, which he shared with Eddie. Paid fifty cents they split, they delivered the handbills old Karl Krutz has run off now and then advertising Big Savings at his East Side ma-and-pa grocery. Delivered some, that is, leaving them on people's porches, and dumped the rest in a trash barrel. They were fired and cussed out pretty good by old Krutz when somebody saw them doing that and snitched on them. Their big aim in life now is to become caddies at the Winatchee Falls Golf & Country Club, where dollar tips for eighteen holes while rare are not unknown, but you have to be sixteen to be a caddy.

So money meanwhile or the lack thereof is and most likely will remain a constant problem, but that's to be expected, middle of The Great Depression. The big mystery is where did all the money go? It didn't just disappear, did it? Somebody must have it, but who? J.P. Morgan and John D. Rockefeller are the principal suspects, but whoever has it, they're keeping it out of circulation. Some Winatchee Falls businesses, the Bugle Call for one, are paying their employes with something called scrip, make-believe money local stores will accept. Some people call this Monopoly money. Monopoly's a new game said to be sweeping the nation. It's really popular, probably because people playing it get to play with make-believe money. The Keefes and the Watoskis, they're sometimes on The Welfare, play it a lot.

Most of these friends are Protestants and Junior Sheeny's a Jew! But Ceil Devlin seems resigned now to the fact that, besides life is hard, the world is full of Protestants and even Jews and she's thankful at any rate there aren't any coons in Eddie's gang. There are only four coons in Winatchee Falls: old Josh Brown, the janitor who mops up at the Bullwhip Bar, and the Washingtons, a couple some people think

T.R. St. George

aren't really married, and their son Booker. The Washingtons live in a big old house with lots of bedrooms on North Broadway near the MSP&P tracks and rent rooms in it to the rare coons visiting Winatchee Falls. The Harlem Globetrotters basketball team on its annual pilgrimage stay there. Booker's the fullback on the Winatchee Falls High football team. He's a big tough kid and a really good football player, so good he probably could go to college and play football if coons went to college. That's what Chesty, the resident expert on many subjects, says anyway.

8.

Thus another long Depression year rolls by and in mid-June Old Charlie Goggins, just turned sixty-three, laid off at the B&P plant in April, dies, and all the Heaney clan, like it or not, find themselves together on a hot humid night in Clement Clarke's Funeral Home in Fairbow, the atmosphere civil enough but somewhat strained, Old Charlie the first member of the elder Heaneys' generation (not counting the three Heaney infants), to die, carried off by esophageal cancer, the alleged hernia he never had an operation for a faulty diagnosis, everybody truly sorry for Gert, widowed at sixty-two, she'll have to move in with Young Charlie, soon to be Old Charlie, and his wife Yegga and their brood—four boys said to be "holy terrors," the oldest soon to be Young Charlie, and another one, boy or girl, on the way—but there's eight years left on the mortgage on her and the late Old Charlie's house, just a house, but no way Gert can keep it, make the mortgage payments, tough to sell too in the middle of The Great Depression, and Gert doesn't get along so good with Yegga, that Bohunk with roots in the mysterious Balkans, not even a Catholic though she's raising the kids Catholic, more or less, and Celeste, Gert and the late Old Charlie's daughter, married with twins somewhere in California but separated from her husband now, won't be coming home for the funeral, can't afford the bus fare, another cross poor Gert will have to bear through all the rest of her days.

All of which Eddie Devlin hears while fooling around with the soon-to-be Young Charlie, six, the oldest holy terror, after ritually kneeling at the late Old Charlie's casket, he looks about the same as he looked alive except thinner, and mumbling, zipping through, a brief prayer for the repose of the late Old Charlie's immortal soul.

The Rosary said and the wake's evening session over, the Timothy J. Heaneys say they have to be getting home, Tim doesn't like to drive at night any more, but Gert won't hear of that. It won't be dark until after nine o'clock, she says, and everybody's supposed to come over to her house for coffee or lemonade and cake and some sandwiches her neighbors made. Which they all do. It's part of the ritual: the Timothy J. Heaneys can't escape it.

They're all sitting around in Gert's stuffy crowded living room pretending to enjoy this repast when Young Charlie—he won't officially be Old Charlie until the late Old Charlie's underground, 260 pounds on the hoof, still a patrolman but up for sergeant if there's ever a vacancy, Yegga says—has the bad taste (or maybe it isn't) to start reminiscing.

"Say, you remember that time, Tim," Young Charlie, he's got a big booming voce, says, "I find your Buick park by the Bus Depot there? Inna No Parking Zone? And I hadda get it towed finally, put it inna the Impound, I dint ever seen you."

Timothy J. Heaney, dapper in a new $20 gray suit and spats, his fringe of now white hair neatly combed, coffee balanced on one knee, gives this some thought—thinks too perhaps at fifty-nine, Ceil surmises later, having just seen the late Old Charlie Goggins laid out in a casket, of his own dwindling mortality. "Yes," at any rate, Timothy J. Heaney says, finally. "I remember that day, Charlie. I wish many times since, Charlie, oh many times I wish, I'd seen you. We'd seen each other. I was here that day, you know. And that night. At the Star Hotel. We'd seen each other, Charlie. . . . Well, I might not caught that bus to Albuquerque. Things might of been different then. . . . Well, no, I guess not. I guess. . . . Oh God, I'm so sorry! So sorry! What I did to all of you! The Estate and all. Everything! We're all together here. It's been

Old Tim's Estate

a long time since we've all been together. I just want you all to know. Nell, Gert, Ceil, Bee, Henry. I am so sorry! Oh so sorry!"

And Timothy J. Heaney begins to cry, bawl, like his old heart's broken, tears rolling down his cheeks, the first grown man Eddie ever really saw cry, grown men at wakes and funerals usually just sniffling some and wiping their eyes.

There's a long silence, everybody sort of embarrassed by this display of emotion, nobody knowing what to do or say. Then Bee jumps up and hugs Tim or tries to, he's still seated, and sort of sobs, she's crying too, "It's all right, Tim. It's all right! It's all over now!"

The holy terror soon to be Young Charlie, racing through the room, bangs into Tim's knees and Tim's coffee goes flying. "Oh hell!" Tim says and stands and Bee, coffee all over the carpet around her feet, gives Tim a proper hug. So, heaving herself from her chair, she's put on weight, does Bergda, she's crying too, and Gert and Nell and Estelle and Edith, all sort of bawling, likewise rise, crowd around Tim and hug him, more or less, all at once. So do Emma Heaney and Ceil finally, though Ceil's just sniffling a little and doesn't hug Tim real tight. Henry Heaney finds one of Tim's hands and pumps it and they all, with the possible exception of Ceil, everybody still sort of bawling and talking at once, tell Tim it's all right, it's all over, ancient history, it wasn't his fault or maybe it was, but it's all over, forgotten now, they're a family at peace again and a family at peace is a wonderful thing and the Lord knows Bee said a lot of Rosaries, hundreds, it finally would happen one day.

Tim wipes his eyes, hugs all his siblings, even Henry, and Bergda and both his daughters and says, though sort of all choked up, "Oh, thank you, thank you! I don't deserve. . . . But thank you. I thank you all from the very bottom of my heart. It's been so long. So hard. . . ." Then just sort of splutters.

Young Charlie whacks the holy terror who ran into Tim and Yegga runs into the kitchen, her big belly bobbing, and gets a towel and mops up the coffee on the rug and on Tim's pants and spats, though Tim says never mind, it doesn't matter, he'll get them dry-cleaned.

"Oh I wish Charlie was here!" Gert says between sobs, "See us all now! He always hated family squabbles. They upset him."

9.

There's always a Heaney Family table at the Fourth of July picnic at Precious Blood now. "Good family get togethers," Bee calls these gatherings, though the games at the 1936 picnic—baseballs flung at bowling pins, hoops tossed over milk bottles, a Fishing Pond for the little kids, Bingo at a nickel a card for the serious gamblers, the big Bingo prize a $2 bag of groceries—do dismally, raising but $121 for the Parish Fuel Fund, many parishioners broke or claiming to be, The Great Depression still raging, no end to it in sight.

Herb Bender's afraid his corn crop, No. 2 Yellow at 14 cents a bushel, won't cover the crop loan he had to get to buy the seed. Henry Heaney's facing a tractor repair Al Morris figures will run close to $30. But Emma Heaney's coming along pretty good after her gallbladder operation: Henry sold six calves, accepting since he had no choice the lousy price the B&P Meat Packing Co. was paying so Emma could go to the Mayo Brothers and had it done right, and Little Tim still has his tonsils and adenoids: Doc Dempsey's second opinion was they aren't so bad they have to come out. Hack and Dick Devlin and their brothers and various other males have a pretty good time discussing the dismal state of the Goddamn Government. Wesley L. Kemp, still driving his Studebaker President but facing an $28 valve job, risking apoplexy, is explosive, volcanic, on that issue. "Goddamn Government's paying farmers more to kill hogs than B&P'll pay for them alive!"

Dick Devlin comes to the Picnic in a new Chrysler Eight

T.R. St. George

demonstrator with white sidewall tires and wire wheels and lets Eddie sit in it for awhile, behind the steering wheel, thrilling Lorrie Stacowitz (though Lorrie unfortunately is not present) with the expert manner in which Speedball Devlin takes the Chrysler through hairpin curves at 100 miles-an-hour.

This good family get together also is marred somewhat when Young Charlie Goggins, the No. 1 holy terror, scratches a T.J.H. off Tim's '27 Buick—but Tim, the day auditor now at the Dobermann Hotel, grits his teeth, says he guesses kids will be kids and won't let Old Charlie, the responsible parent, pay for the damage. Old Charlie, a sergeant, finally promoted a month ago, 280 pounds on the hoof, offers to pay but also notes that the Fairbow Police Department is on two-thirds pay now, Fairbow just about broke in the middle of The Great Depression.

"I guess," Ceil Devlin says on their way home to Winatchee Falls, zipping along in the gathering dusk at 35 mph in the new (used) '29 Model A Ford Hack bought a month ago off Cheesy Adams' Used Lot for $195 with his employee discount, "Tim's still trying to make it up. The Estate and all. Any little way he can."

But Ceil's not really bitter any more. Time heals. Hack's in line for the next day job at the Day & Night Garage. She was elected second vice-president of The Friends of the Public Library at The Friends' annual meeting, which means she'll be the president eight years hence or sooner if old Mrs. Brumhalter the president and Lucinda Gottery the first vice-president die or resign or move away. She has her eye on a nice two-bedroom unit in the College Apartments, a regular apartment building on the near West Side. And Eddie's getting pretty good grades in his freshman year at Winatchee Falls High. Ceil thinks he should start the Commercial Course when he's a junior, fit himself for a job when he graduates since, though she doesn't mention the vanished Estate, it's unlikely, no end to The Great Depression in sight, there'll ever be any money for college.

This is fine with Eddie, who's mainly counting the days until he's fifteen and can get his driving permit and start driving the Model A

Old Tim's Estate

under Hack's supervision. He never did give much serious thought to the $250 once earmarked for his "advanced schooling" in Old Tim's Heaney's Last Will & Testament and also doubts he'll be a teetotal—doubts he is a teetotal any longer by Old Tim's harsh standards. He drinks a little beer now and then. Chesty Bennett, a consummate thief, sometimes swipes a bottle of 3.2 right out of the cooler at old Krutz's ma-and-pa grocery while Eddie keeps old Krutz—who seems to have forgotten the handbill business—busy at the candy counter. They drink this beer and smoke the Old Gold cigarettes Chesty swipes from his mother, Chesty's taught Eddie to inhale, while sitting in the sun or the shade, depending on the weather, beside the high tin fence around Sheeny's Junkyard, meanwhile studying the dirty little comic books Chesty swipes from under the counter at Hub Horlick's Cigar Store. Eddie knows where babies come from now and how they get there and that there's a lot more to this business than just making babies , many variations graphically depicted in the little comic books.

Chesty claims to know a girl, Annie Seaver, she's seventeen and a junior and lives on Eighth Avenue on the East Side, who will take off all her clothes and let guys look at her naked—if she's home alone and in the mood. Her dad owns a dry-cleaning place and works nights a lot since he had to let his presser go and her ma's a call-in waitress at the Princess Cafe nights there's a Bowling League dinner or something. Chesty often says they should go over and see Annie some night when she's home alone and in the mood, but she's not been home alone, or said she wasn't anyway, the six or seven times they've phoned her house.

Eddie's not quite sure he's ready for that in any case, though he thinks about it a lot. It certainly sounds like an Occasion of Sin, another springboard for the deadly Unclean Thoughts he now embraces and enjoys and, risking Hell, makes no determined effort, or any effort at all, to put from his mind. Annie Seaver, a plump blonde girl he sees now and then in school, fully clothed, is frequently a marquee player in these Unclean Thoughts. It used to be Lorrie Stacowitz, also blonde and sort of plump, who slowly took off all her clothes in these

173

Unclean Thoughts and looked finally, bare naked, a lot like a fat blonde darn near bare naked girl displaying her charms in a recent Police Gazette. But Eddie, not without regret, has pretty much written Lorrie off—been spurned by Lorrie, in fact. They share a Study Hall period but Lorrie sits on the far side of the room (also the school auditorium) with the juniors. Eddie, however, discovered where Lorrie hangs her coat outside her homeroom and left a note in her coat pocket. It was sort of poetic, rhymed anyway. Hi there Lorrie! How are things these days in Stiles? Tell me all the news. Leave a note in your coat. E.T. Devlin. Lorrie left a note in her coat, another rhyme. Don't you, you little jerk, ever leave another note in my coat! L.S.

But the world's full of girls. Many in Study Hall already have chests Chesty calls bazooms, boobs, jugs, jars, etc. Annie Seaver's jugs are stupendous. So are Margie Bremer's all at once, considering she's only fourteen. Margie's also a Winatchee Falls High freshman and so is Buddy Douglas, once Eddie best friend in Stiles though that friendship's lapsed. Eddie shares no classes with Buddy or Margie and they sit rows away in Study Hall: it's not arranged alphabetically. They still live in Stiles and ride to and from school with Margie's dad, Werner, the failed bootlegger, the car-wash man now at T.J. (Slippery) Hanrahan's Oldsmobile Pontiac and Chevy dealership and garage on South Broadway, in the weary '29 Chevy that Werner bought used from Slippery with his employee discount. Werner, this a report from a deadbeat who still owes Hack Devlin $12, got out of the Leavenworth Prison after nine months with three months off for Good Behavior, his debt to society paid in full, and was on the WPA for two years, leaning on a shovel, then, another lucky man in the middle of The Great Depression, latched onto the car-wash job.

Evylee Hanrahan's jugs are pretty big too. She's Slippery's only offspring, sort of short but full packed, with long dark hair, another freshman transfer from Holy Redeemer ducking Latin. But Eddie never did get acquainted with Evylee at Holy Redeemer and, though they're both in Miss Gossman's English class, she's evinced no interest in improving their acquaintance. She's had no role in the

Old Tim's Estate

Unclean Thoughts Department. Chesty, who keeps track of these things, says Evylee's going steady with Archie Haber Jr., a junior and the No.2 center on the basketball team. Archie's old man, Arthur Haber Sr., another rich man, owns the Haber Construction Co., which, never mind The Great Depression, built an addition to the Pretzell Chiropractic Clinic a year ago and, this truly amazing, a weatherproof tunnel for people called a "subway," lined with tan tile and dimly lit, underneath West College Street between The Chiro and the Dobermann Hotel. Many local residents consider this subway the Ninth Wonder of the World. Others think it pretty silly. True Midwesterners only go underground when confronted by cyclones. The effete Easterners now trickling into The Chiro use this subway though, even when the weather's good. It's supposed to be reserevd for Chiro patients and Dobermann Hotel guests but sneaking into it and through it and out of it without getting caught is a popular new game for Winatchee Falls juveniles. Chesty often leads these expeditions.

The Chiro's doing pretty well despite the Great Depression. Its fame has spread and a farmer (or effete Easterner) with a bad back—Chesty, quoting his mother Pauline the physical therapist, says—will if their back gets bad enough sell some pigs or cows or something (or bonds) to finance a trip to and treatment at The Chiro.

Chesty also says, though he may be lying, he's squeezed Annie Seaver's bare boobs with his bare hands and tells Eddie all about that every time they see Annie, fully clothed, in school or on the street. These sightings often trigger deadly Unclean Thoughts.

"So, are you abusing yourself, then?" The Rev. Bernie (Penance) Griffin, a full-fledged priest now, one of the assistant pastors at Holy Redeemer, a grim avenging figure in a black cassock seen dimly through the screen in the confessional, says when Eddie, propelled by Ceil, goes to Confession.

"Mmmm glrrb mmmm," is what Eddie, afraid to tell a full-fledged priest an outright lie in the sacred confines of the confessional, dim though the light be, mumbles. The Rev. Griffin goes on then about how bad this makes God feel and so on and lays on the penance. Eddie sometimes finds it hard to believe the Deity's high spirits and peace of mind apparently depend on one half-grown boy's ability to suppress all his normal animal urges—but that's the way it is, apparently. You'd think the Deity would worry more about the typhoons, floods, famines, earthquakes, volcanic eruptions etc. briefly noted in the Bugle Call that more or less regularly kill thousands and thousands of people in China or India or Afghanistan or someplace. Maybe not though. Those people weren't Catholics. They were all going Straight to Hell anyway.

Eddie of course does not pick The Rev. Griffin for a confessor if he can help it, or The Rev. Brent (Bent Willie) Williams either, the other assistant pastor, who also goes heavy on the penance and, this another report from Chesty, likes to pinch altar boys' butts. No kid with any sense picks Penance Griffin or Bent Willie. Holy Redeemer has three confessionals and the first step, going to Confession, is to ask some kid who's already been, "Which one's O'Herlihy in?" The Rt. Rev. Desmond O'Herlihy's the pastor at Holy Redeemer. He's darn near seventy-five, half deaf, he's heard so many Confessions, so many sins, there's nothing he's not heard before a hundred times and goes easy on the penance. Three Hail Marys usually for anything short of first-degree murder or missing Mass on Sunday and a practicing Catholic can rip those off in twelve seconds flat.

Some kids of course, though just absolved of all their sins, promptly sin again, lying when asked, Which one's O'Herlihy in? Then Eddie winds up with Penance Griffin or Bent Willie, who often hand out for a penance a whole Rosary!

Wolfe (Woofie) Strudel—the mean kid whose pitching whipped Stiles 21-2 and whiffed Eddie four times in that 1929 school picnic softball game—often lies and so does sneaky Ignatius (Ignatz) Malone the undertaker's son. Woofie lives in Winatchee Falls now: he's a Winatchee Falls High senior. The Simpson cheese factory where his dad Herman was the cheese-maker "went under" as the saying goes early in The Great Depression, but the Strudels survived. Herman's a

Old Tim's Estate

cheese-maker's help at the Co-Op Dairy now and Woofie, the lucky stiff, has a part-time job helping his Uncle Helmut in Helmut's one-truck trucking business. Woofie still comes to Mass every other Sunday with his mother (the Burns girl who was supposed to marry Dick Devlin) and his little sister and goes to Confession now and then. Eddie doubts Woofie ever confesses he's half a Lutheran, though.

Ignatz Malone's the head altar boy, the one who caught Chesty sampling the sacramental wine and got Chesty fired. His dad owns the Malone Funeral Home on Fourth Street but Ignatz, Chesty says, is afraid of dead people. Ignatz also, this another report from Chesty, likes it when Bent Willie pinches his butt. Chesty's thankful Ignatz got him fired but he's pretty sure Ignatz is one of those mysterious detested sexual perverts everybody calls a "fruit. Big Russ Schneider the East Side bully thought so too. Russ, so the story goes, once tied Ignatz to the Hawthorne Playground cyclone fence and said he was going to cut Ignatz's pecker off—but the school janitor, old Janny Jansen, heard Ignatz screaming and intervened.

"One thing though, you're Catholic," this another thing Chesty often says following a sketchy Confession, "It's a lot of work, but you go to Confession, say your penance, whole Rosary you have to, and you're all set. It's like you wipe stuff off a blackboard, y'know, clean slate, and you can start out all over again, have some fun."

Chesty's quite a guy. He started smoking, he says, when he was twelve, drinking beer when he was thirteen and he may be, Eddie thinks, blessed. Blessed meaning he has some of the really scary mysterious powers Eddie came across in a book about necromancy in the Public Library—Eddie's a reader now, pleasing Ceil, has his own library card. Chesty at any rate frequently catches one of the toads that live in the grass beside the tin fence around Sheeny's Junkyard—a sure way to get warts, that a well-known scientific fact—and tortures it for awhile with a cigarette, but has no visible warts.

Chesty also has a pretty sweet life. Pauline, his divorced (or not divorced) mother—she's pretty old, about thirty-five, and a little bit fat but still pretty good-looking—goes out nights with boyfriends and doesn't seem to care a whole lot, what Chesty does or where he goes so long as he's home when she gets home and maintains a B average on his report cards. Which Chesty does. He swiped some blank report cards once when he was in the principal's office for not wearing a necktie under his crew-neck sweater (Winatchee Falls High has a "dress code" and neckties are part of it) and fills these cards out himself, Bs and an honest A in Phy Ed. Chesty's a pretty good swimmer from having spent parts of seven summers diving for golf balls in the Winatchee River and darn near an eighty-percent free throw shooter. He'd go out for the basketball team if he was taller and there wasn't a rule the athletes don't dare smoke.

Pauline's a lot different than Ceil. Eddie sometimes wishes Pauline was his mother but feels guilty afterwards, when he think that. Ceil, he assumes, though rarely giving this much thought, loves him in her way—she has to, she's his mother—and he knows, she often tells him this, she really hopes he'll do well in life. Get good marks in school, stay out of trouble, get a good steady job some day, always have enough money, more than she's had anyway, and more happiness, and always go to Mass on Sundays and the Holy Days of Obligation. But she often seems fraught with doubt about his future and, she also says, worries a lot when he's out running around with that Bennett boy, doing the Lord knows what. Ceil of course doesn't know Chesty smokes and steals beer or that Eddie drinks this beer. She'd have a fit if she did know and no doubt tell Eddie his grandfather, Old Tim Heaney the teetotaler, "must be spinning in his grave!"

In fact, Eddie doesn't much like beer, the way it tastes, but always drinks some when Chesty steals a bottle. Chesty's a peer who applies a lot of pressure.

TO BE CONTINUED

NORMANDALE COMMUNITY COLLEGE
LIBRARY
9700 FRANCE AVENUE SOUTH
BLOOMINGTON, MN 55431-4399

Printed in the United States
35770LVS00002B